THE BEIJING OF POSSIBILITIES

 STORIES

JONATHAN TEL

FOREWORD BY HELAN XIAO

OTHER PRESS

NEW YORK

Poetry excerpt on page 147 from "Wang Zhaojun (two poems),"
by Bai Juyi, translated by Burton Watson. First published in
Renditions, Nos. 59 & 60 (2003), pp. 46–49. Reprinted by
permission of the Research Centre for Translation,
The Chinese University of Hong Kong.

Two of the stories in this collection were originally published as follows:
"The Beijing of Possibilities" (*Zoetrope: All-Story*)
"Rise Upward to the Blue Clouds" (*Prospect Magazine*, UK)

Production Editor: Yvonne E. Cárdenas
Book design: Simon M. Sullivan

This book was set in 12.25 pt Centaur
by Alpha Design & Composition

Photographs by Jonathan Tel

10 9 8 7 6 5 4 3 2 1

Library of Congress Cataloging-in-Publication Data

Tel, Jonathan.
The Beijing of possibilities / Jonathan Tel ; with a foreword by Helan Xiao.
p. cm.
ISBN 978-1-59051-326-2 (acid-free paper) — ISBN 978-1-59051-347-7 (electronic
text) 1. Beijing (China)—Fiction. 2. Short stories, American. I. Title.
PS3620.E44B45 2009
813'.6—dc22
2009000275

To Elizabeth Hollander

To have friends come from afar, is this not a delight?
—THE ANALECTS OF CONFUCIUS

CONTENTS

CONTENTS

BEIJING IS THE CENTER of the universe. Ask anybody who lives there. "The true Beijinger secretly believes that people living anywhere else have to be, in some sense, kidding."

Humans have been making their home hereabouts for a quarter of a million years, but it was in 1267 that Kublai Khan, the Mongol king and interlocutor of Marco Polo, created a city in his image. He chose a location to the northeast of China's center of gravity, within dreaming distance of the steppes. A nomad, a rider of horses, he saw no reason to have his capital lie by any river—a distinction Beijing shares with Jerusalem. Then as now, every spring yellow dust blows in from beyond the Great Wall—last gasp of the Mongol hordes.

In 1403 Yongle—the Ming emperor, a despot whose name translates as Perpetual Happiness—moved his capital from the south to Beijing. At the heart of it, the Forbidden City—a concrete demonstration of Confucianism: power devolves from the center. He devised a system of tributes in which wealth funneled in from across the country. People came where the money was; soon Beijing was the most populous city in the world.

And in 2008 the Olympics arrived in a metropolis of extraordinary variety; migrants from throughout the nation, speaking many dialects, are drawn here, seeking, among difficulties and dangers, a kind of freedom, an erotic excitement, not to be found in the provinces. Even we who were born here are migrants of a sort, moving in a world that we as children could scarcely have dreamed of. The old pieties of Communism and Confucianism are still half-believed in, as are the new ones of Self-Reliance and Money. The model citizen is the Monkey King—a do-gooder who is also a trickster, a patriot who seeks foreign wisdom, a victim who triumphs over his adversaries.

The Olympics, as well as being a manifestation of civic pride, brought an awareness that Beijing was being observed from afar. (It would never have crossed Kublai Khan's or Yongle's mind to care about the opinion of outsiders.) Which leads to the kind of self-consciousness that enables and demands fiction. Like all great cities, it exists as much in imagination as in reality. The Beijing of Possibilities—let there be a guidebook to that.

—Helan Xiao

PREFACE

I CAME TO BEIJING in 1988. I was researching Ming dynasty literature, and in my imagination the modern city was superimposed on the city of centuries past. China grew on me, and I was caught up in the changes that were then taking place—not least thanks to my friendship with the poet Helan Xiao. In the decades since, I've returned as often as I can.

I've lived in many places since—London, Jerusalem, Tokyo, New York—and have written about them, mostly in fiction.

Helan and I lost touch—until she contacted me last year, inviting me to assist with the translation of her acclaimed collection of stories set in contemporary Beijing. The book had originally been published under a pseudonym, but in the light of a much-publicized affair (a relationship with a software entrepreneur; in the divorce proceedings the wife cited Helan's fiction as proof of her moral turpitude) there is no longer any point in masking the author's identity. Helan has contributed a foreword to this edition, and I have taken the liberty of adding a concluding chapter, narrating certain episodes in her life. For any misrepresentations, and for any errors that may have crept into my adaptation of her work, I alone, of course, am wholly responsible.

—Jonathan Tel

THE BEIJING OF POSSIBILITIES

YEAR OF THE GORILLA

IT'S BEEN A WHILE since the Monkey King set out on his Journey to the West. With his Fiery-Gazing Golden Eyes he infallibly recognized Evil, and vowed to combat it in every form. He changed shape at will and leaped from cloud to cloud. It was in the spring of 2008 that the Gorillagram appeared in mainland China. (One of those fads, we believe, that snuck in from America or Europe.) A Taiwanese-owned company introduced the concept; they were in the business of couriering documents around Beijing, and they diversified—or call it a promotional gimmick. The way it works is that a man in a gorilla suit arrives in your building. He steps out of the elevator and jogs right up to the reception desk, banging his chest. He's directed to the appropriate cubicle, where he sings, "Happy Birthday to You!" to the lucky and amazed recipient, or "Congratulations on your Promotion! Ten thousand Congratulations!" He accepts his tip and off he goes.

So who is he, this fellow in the furry disguise? His true name is unknown; no doubt he's a migrant worker, not legally resident in the capital. The salary is pitiful, and the costume hot and itchy; he must be from the South. He's not as tall as he looks: his real eyes are at the level of the Gorilla's snout, and he speaks through a veil around its throat. Six days a week, he cycles around Beijing, going wherever he's told; sometimes he's in a hell of a rush, pedaling like crazy, scarcely time to pant his song before he dashes to the next appointment; but there's downtime too—he un-Velcros his head and puffs a cigarette. There are worse ways to make a living.

Now one afternoon in June he'd just finished a job singing the Retirement Song at a graphic design company on Qianmen Dajie, and he was about to mount his Forever bicycle which he'd parked in a nearby alley—not really a rough area, though you have to watch out for pickpockets. A businesswoman walked by, a red handbag swinging from her shoulder. Suddenly he heard a roar and a Honda moped was accelerating past, two men on it. The passenger grabbed the handbag! The businesswoman screamed; she clung to her strap. For what can't have been more than a few seconds the man and the woman struggled. She would not let go. Then the Honda sped down to the end of the alley and made a sharp left. The Gorilla was shocked— he'd heard about such things, he'd been warned by his boss to be careful, and whenever he left his bicycle he always locked it to a railing—but he'd never witnessed such a blatant attempt. So the big city is as dangerous as they say.

While he was thinking these thoughts, the familiar and ominous roar recurred. Once again the thieves were in the alley! They'd circled around, and were swooping in for another go! This time both crooks reached out to seize the prize; the driver kept one hand on his vehicle while with the other he pawed the woman's strap, and his accomplice punched her on the breasts.

As for the Gorilla—a timid man, normally—he couldn't bear to see a woman treated like this. He let go of his Forever and bounded along the alley, beating his fists against the front of his costume and uttering a deep "Hoo-hoo!" The thieves had already taken possession of the handbag and were about to drive off. The Gorilla pounced. With one hairy arm he practically choked the driver, with the other he twisted the handlebars, knocking the moped over, while his knee connected with the groin of the whimpering accomplice. He dusted off the handbag and returned it to the businesswoman. The thieves fled. The Gorilla made a little bow.

He returned to his bicycle and headed off to his next job.

That might have been the end of the matter, but it so happened that a student in a nearby teashop had heard the noise and stepped outside. He took photographs of the incident with his cell phone. He posted an account on his blog.

The blog was linked to other blogs—and soon the pictures, along with cut-and-pastings of the text and retellings of the story, appeared on several online forums. There was much speculation as to who the Gorilla might have been, along with approval of his actions, as well as more wide-ranging discussion of the growing problem of urban street crime. (Who is to blame? What should we do about it?) The story was picked up by a newspaper in Hebei Province, and from there it was copied by a news agency and printed in further papers and magazines. BRAVE GORILLA RESCUES CITIZEN—IN HER PLIGHT, AN "ANIMAL" HELPS HER—SUPERMONKEY TO THE RESCUE! Given that there was only one Gorillagram company in Beijing, it wasn't difficult for the media to locate the Gorilla. But the management turned down all requests for interviews on his behalf. It would draw attention away from their core business; the last thing they wanted was for the public to think they were in the business of crime-fighting, not to speak of the potential liability suit. They handed the Gorilla his fan mail—letters and postcards from all across the nation, including a proposal of marriage from a young lady in Shaanxi Province, addressed simply to Hero Gorilla, Beijing—and told him sternly to stick to his job in the future. From the Gorilla's point of view, he was more embarrassed than anything; all he'd done was what you or I might under the circumstances. And it made his work harder. When he went into an office to do his act, likely as not the middle managers would want to chat and the secretaries would flirt, and he didn't get bigger tips either— on the contrary, people seemed to assume now he was a celebrity he didn't need the money. "Excuse me," he'd mumble in his Southern accent, "it was over in a second, I don't remember much." And if they still kept pestering him he'd deny his involvement: "I guess you must be thinking of some other ape."

Meanwhile the online discussion continued. The majority of netizens were supportive of his actions ("We need monkeys like that in Guangdong" and "The government ought to award the Gorilla a medal" were typical responses; a woman who called herself Tingting23 said she'd been born in the Year of the Monkey herself and "Monkeys are famous for their helpfulness and quick thinking"). But others were skeptical: "How do we know the Gorilla was in fact a hero? All we can tell from the pictures is that two men were taking a woman's handbag and the Gorilla intervened. Maybe she *wanted* the men to have her bag?" The story was alluded to on a discussion board: "It is a shame that sticks-in-the-mud are opposing a market economy with Chinese characteristics. The last thing we need is to have a Gorilla barge in every time we shake hands on a deal!" Which led to further criticism, as well as some support of the Gorilla for "preserving Maoist values." An editorial in the July issue of the *Beijing Financial Review* referred somewhat obscurely to "Gorillas and their ilk who shoot sparrows with a pearl" in the context of defending the opening up of the mining industry to foreign investment.

That summer, in advance of the Olympics, security teams were going around the city checking IDs, arresting or deporting illegals. Those who made their living on the streets were especially in danger of being caught, and many jugglers and conjurors and balloon-folders were never seen again. The Gorilla felt fairly secure: with a getup so striking, he didn't look like he had anything to hide. But one afternoon when he came back to the courier company, a police officer was waiting for him. "We've had reports," the officer said. The Gorilla said, "What did I do?" The officer fastened handcuffs around his thick hairy wrists and drove him to the station.

Now it seemed that every officer in Beijing was gathered around, eager to ogle the celebrity; the police were pointing and chattering among themselves like children at the zoo. They yelled questions at him. "Where's your ID? Where's your temporary residence permit? Where's your employment permit?" The Gorilla shook his head. A middle-ranking officer scolded him, "You're the worst kind. What we call a Three-No."

There followed the business of taking fingerprints; it wasn't possible to bare his hand without taking off his entire costume, and in the end an officer just pressed the Gorilla's furry fingers on the ink pad. Next he was photographed, face-on and in profile, for the record. He asked, "Do you want me to remove my head?" But he was pictured just as he was—nobody wanted to see the face of an ordinary human migrant worker; let's not break the spell.

"I didn't know I was doing anything bad," the Gorilla pleaded. "All I did was go around offices singing songs. I'll sing for you, if you like."

That was the wrong thing to have said. One officer responded, "What does he think this is? Karaoke night?" Another went,

"Sing? You think we can't sing for ourselves, better than any monkey?" A third declared, "Are you attempting to bribe a police officer in the course of his duties?" while making the "shame on you" gesture with index finger against cheek. And meanwhile the first officer was repeating his witticism, laughing at the punchline—"*Karaoke night!*"—louder every time.

A senior officer, Detective Wang, held out his hands for silence. He took charge of the interrogation. "Listen. Gorilla, Mister Monkey, whoever you are. According to our records, you were involved in the theft of a handbag."

"The handbag wasn't actually stolen. What happened was—"

"Aha! You're admitting it was a case of attempted theft!"

The Gorilla tried to explain, but his Mandarin was far from fluent, and it was difficult to raise his voice above the background noise. An older officer was warbling "My Motherland" in a resonant tenor—"*When friends visit we treat them well; when enemies visit we are ready for them with a hunting musket . . .*"—and a younger officer was marveling, "We've never had a monkey in here before." Detective Wang glared at the audience, "Shush! I'm trying to conduct an interrogation here!"

The Gorilla mumbled his excuses.

Detective Wang wiped his brow with the back of his hand. This was really too much. He couldn't be expected to arrest every beggar, busker, and queerly costumed oddball in the city. He scrolled down the Gorilla's file—pages of barely relevant stuff trawled up by a search engine. "So, Gorilla, is it true that you're opposed to the development of capitalist enterprise in China?"

"Yes. I mean, no. Er, what is the correct answer?"

The station had never been so crowded. Still more police were coming in to gawk, and civilian employees too. One officer had texted his girlfriend, who'd come running over in high heels from the fashion boutique where she was employed; another officer had brought his aged mother, who jabbed her fingers in the Gorilla's direction and stifled her laughter with a hand over her toothless mouth.

Wang turned to an underling, Detective Zhao. "Oh, get him to confess something, then we'll get rid of him."

Wang sat down at a desk with his back to the fray, and busied himself with paperwork. Meanwhile Zhao typed the confession on the Gorilla's behalf. "Actions liable to cause public disorder . . . Obstruction of the highway . . . Failure to show Identity Document when requested . . ."

"I don't know how to read all these fancy words," the Gorilla said. "And besides, I'm innocent."

"Yes, yes," said Zhao, and pressed the Gorilla's thumbprint on the dotted line.

The Gorilla was in the midst of the mob. Some wit kept offering him a banana, another taunted him, "Where's your demon-exposing mirror, Monkey King?" and people climbed on chairs and on the radiator, the better to peek and jabber at the suspect, and all the while he slumped there, surrounded by his enemies and admirers, saying nothing at all.

Then somebody made a dunce's cap out of cardboard and put it on the Gorilla's head, and a placard was strung around his neck, I OPPOSED THE WILL OF THE PEOPLE, and he was made to stand with arms twisted back in "airplane position" for a full hour, his secret eyes weeping behind the simian snout, while the police drank tea and had their photos taken with the captive beast.

Eventually, "You can go now," Detective Wang said. And a young officer patted his fur and murmured, "Soft."

The Gorilla went back to the courier company. He did some more jobs for them, cycling to offices and singing congratulations, but his heart wasn't in it. A couple of weeks later, soon after the closing ceremony for the Olympics, he failed to arrive at work. The gorilla suit remained empty, sagging on the hook. The company considered hiring a replacement, but the fad had had its day, and really it was more trouble than it was worth. As for the man who had acted the part, we can only guess his fate. Is he still in Beijing, in a different guise, working in some other line? Or did he return to the village he grew up in? At any rate the Hero Gorilla has never been seen again.

THE BOOK OF AUSPICIOUS AND INAUSPICIOUS DREAMS

AT LAST THEY HAD A PLACE of their own. At the beginning of 2008 a young couple, the Songs, moved into an apartment in the Haidian district of Beijing. The location was fashionable. The price was reasonable because—though adjacent to lofty postmodern structures—their building was bland and stubby, a mere four stories, dating back to the 1960s. The apartment had been remodeled several times since, and needed more work. Which was fine by them. Do It Yourself!—that was the slogan they kept chanting to each other. They'd met at university and both spent their professional lives in front of a computer— he was in software and she was a graphic designer—but his father ran a plumbing business in Chongqing while her parents were peasants in Guangxi Province. Laboring with one's hands—they honored what their ancestors had done, since the beginning of time.

They loved their home, what it was and what it might become. Bedroom, living room, bathroom, kitchen, another room which would be her study (the plan was to put his desk in the bedroom), and one more room in the corner, cramped, its only window little and high, not much use for anything now, though if they ever had a child . . . They dreamed of virtual apartments, and she printed out a blueprint showing how things ought to be.

The priority was furniture. Much of what had come with the place could stay. The bed, its headboard carved in a dragon design, was older than the building (how on earth had it been brought up here?) and qualified as an antique. The couch and dinner table dated from the Deng Xiaoping era. But they urgently needed computer desks and chairs. One weekend in January, beating the Chinese New Year rush, they "went on vacation to Sweden," as they put it. They borrowed a friend's Toyota pickup and drove to Ikea. They made an afternoon of it, eating meatballs in the restaurant and enjoying the gratis coffee and Wi Fi. In addition to furniture, they selected napkins and tablecloths, flatware and glassware and silverware.

Cups and plates left behind by the previous occupants— these they threw out, but they kept a set of chopstick rests found in a drawer, also an oxblood china bowl which they placed on a side table and arranged apples in.

An alarm clock with a picture of Mao on its face turned up under the sink. It didn't work (the time was forever ten o'clock) but they valued it for its funky retro appeal, and installed it on the shelf above the toilet, next to a paperback of the Duke of Zhao's *Book of Auspicious and Inauspicious Dreams*.

They hung an octagonal mirror opposite the entrance.

They brought home a pot of wisteria, to keep indoors for the season. One day soon it would flourish on the balcony and climb hopefully over the railing.

The husband, Song Tao, took on responsibility for installing an up-to-date shower. Song Haiping checked that the wiring was up to code, with the help of an ex-boyfriend of hers who had a master's in electrical engineering; Tao paid him with a bottle of Johnnie Walker.

The grandest task they put off. A necessary destruction. The wall between the smallest room and the living room, that had to go. "We'll make ourselves an L-shaped living room! It'll be full of light!"

She said, "Suppose we need the little room after all, one day?"

"Then we'll put in a folding screen."

It was on March 8, International Women's Day, that they took up the challenge. Appropriate timing for a new start, she thought. Outside, icicles were dripping from the eaves but the throbbing radiator was making the interior if anything too hot. They covered the furniture with dust sheets and spread newspaper on the floor. Tao whistled the anthem "*Women have strong arms . . .*" "Hey, shouldn't you be the one doing all the work?"

"We use our strong arms to make men work for us."

He stripped to the waist. "I like showing off my muscles for a cute three-eight"—self-consciously using hip slang.

She bit her lower lip at him.

Both put on Tyvek coveralls—a dull white, the color of mourning. Then face masks, the medical kind with a loop behind each ear, as if they were about to amputate a limb. Goggles, next. He fitted his hands into work gloves.

She said, "We're a hundred percent sure it's not load-bearing, right?"

"Right." He tapped the wall—a hollow sound. "A junky partition like that? I could push it over with my pinky."

He lifted the rented sledgehammer . . .

But even as it swung through the air, this thought was shared: there was some possibility, however slight, the wall might be load-bearing after all—and along with the wall the entire ceiling would come tumbling down; and the apartment of the Chang family upstairs would fall into theirs, squashing their home out of existence.

He'd hardly dented it.

Grunted. Levered back for another go.

"Ah," she said.

A cloud of dust. When it cleared, it was evident he'd chipped the wall—this much and no more.

A third time, putting all he had into it—aiming not for the surface but the far side. A multiple cracking noise—a dust fog, splinters falling.

"Yes, yes!" she said. "Oh that feels so good!"

And with a force he'd never known he possessed he brought the sledgehammer down, demolishing the feeble plasterboard, which crashed and fell like an idol.

"Oh, Tao!"

"Oh, Haiping!"

Dust everywhere; the couple coughed and blinked. Rubble on newspaper. Shafts of milky light shone into the new L-shaped living room, illuminating the sweating, panting man and the woman hugging him. She unzipped her Tyvek and pressed his goggled, masked head against her breasts.

Little time to play. There was work ahead of them. Later the ceiling would need to be sanded and repainted. Later still, they would rearrange their furniture in accord with the new-born space, improve the feng shui. But first things first. They crouched and picked up the larger fragments of plaster, throw-ing them in a trash can.

It was then that they both saw—in the space where the wall had been—an object. Cylindrical, low rather than tall. He brushed it with his gloved hand. A tin box with a peeling label, *Preserved Longans, Product of "Emulate Lei Feng" Factory No. 2*, with a design of marching workers and peasants. "Where in heaven did that descend from?" She mimed an act of spitting to drive off evil spirits while he declared, "It was inside the wall all along."

When he shook it, it rattled.

"Open it, Tao."

But the lid, rusted, wouldn't budge. Next she tugged— no joy.

Let nothing stand in the way of a loving young couple. By dint of banging and prying with a nail file, three screwdrivers, and a teaspoon, and a series of joint efforts involving the hus-band gripping the base while the wife massaged the top, the operation was carried to success.

This is what the Songs found inside the tin:

• A Leica camera
• A harmonica

- A pair of pince-nez
- A naval compass, brass-bound
- A postcard showing Hong Kong harbor in 1962
- Thirty-three black-and-white photographs
- A jade spoon
- Two calligraphy brushes and a little jar of congealed ink
- *Fleurs du mal*, in a 1938 translation
- A piano score of "Für Elise"

With due formality they sat down on the draped chairs and spread the contents of the tin on the draped table. They unmasked and degoggled. They leafed through the photographs. *Carte de visite* of a pigtailed gentleman in *chang pao*. Close-up of a young lady—heavy Qing dynasty makeup and an as-you-wish collar. A man wearing a fedora and a fur-trimmed overcoat. The same man in a Japanese robe. A woman in a peony-pattern dress, holding the hand of a long-haired infant; underexposed. A young couple at a costume ball: she a ballerina and he a shaggy beast from the neck down.

No need to say it out loud. There was only one plausible explanation as to why this cache had been hidden. She tapped the compass: its arrow quivered and resumed pointing north. Throughout its time in the wall, the compass had been secretly controlled by the earth's magnetism.

In an attempt to dissipate the tension Tao horsed around. He mimicked the pompous expression of the fellow in the *carte de visite*, extending his fingers next to his nape as if his hair extended in a queue. In the style of the dialogue of TV historical dramas: "It is the will of the Emperor that we scorn the barbarian tribute."

"The Empress decrees we post the tribute on eBay." She dropped back into her normal voice. "Seriously, Tao, what will we do with this stuff?"

"We should return it to whoever put it there, of course." His gaze met hers. "Or their heirs."

She quoted her grandmother, "If you cook dumplings in a teapot, they won't come out through the spout"—and repeated the saying, translating it from Guangxi dialect. Husband and wife spoke fluent Mandarin but it was the mother tongue of neither; there were things they could never communicate in words.

A few minutes of debate and they came to a compromise: they'd exercise due diligence in seeking the original owner. If that failed, they'd sell the lot for what they could get.

They e-mailed the previous resident, a soil biologist now teaching at an agricultural college in Yunnan Province, but he was of little help. "I moved in four years ago. I bought the apartment from a man named Wang Wei, who emigrated to Canada, he'd been living there a few years." That seemed a dead end. Even if they could track down Wang Wei (a common name, hard to find on a search engine), how likely was it he'd know who'd lived here decades before?

The following Monday Tao was telecommuting from home while his wife went to her office. More out of boredom than addiction, he headed out at lunchtime to buy a pack of cigarettes at the store opposite; he let an elderly blind man go ahead of him. The man bought a single Baisha, and Tao offered him a light. "My wife and I recently moved into Long Life Apartments, Grandfather."

"Ah. The building with the arch in front of it—"

"What arch?" Tao said, but the man was saying, "—with a dragon on the lintel." (Tao recalled two slabs of stone on the sidewalk, which could well have been the base of an arched gate before the road had been widened.) "The dragon'll beat off any foul demons, eh?"

Tao said, "Have you lived in this district long?"

"I was born here! Year of the Monkey. What year are you?"

"I'm Ox. And my wife is Monkey, like yourself."

"Ha, you know what they say: Monkey jumps on the back of Ox! My late wife was a Rat. The astrologer said we'd be compatible, and we were."

Belatedly they exchanged their full names. Tao gave the name of his wife also.

"Ah, so you both come from families with the same name. In the old days, that would have been considered unlucky."

"But no one thinks that anymore." Tao sucked in deep and blew a plume of smoke across the smoke of the old man. "Do you by any chance know who lived in our place—Apartment 23—back in the late sixties or early seventies?"

"Apartment 23 . . . 23, ah?" The blind man fiddled with his stick as he pondered, gently rapping the earth. "Oh yes. That would be the Ji family. Mr. Ji died in—let me see, the year I had my glaucoma—1959, and his wife, her name was Liu, she lived on her own till the mid-eighties. Then she moved in with her niece, out by Xizhimen Bridge."

"Do you have any more information about her, Grandfather?"

"I might. Come with me."

They walked along the shopping street and down an alley. The blind man's home was an iron-roofed shack. A mattress lay diagonally across the floor; he groped expertly underneath and pulled out a tattered notebook. "It's in there somewhere."

The young man looked through the book. There it was, faded but legible, a list of names and telephone numbers. "Liu" jumped out at him. He copied the information into his cell phone.

As he was about to leave, the blind man said, "I'm a masseur. Does your neck hurt? Your skull? Your liver? Your kidney? Your feet? I take away pains and aches. Very cheap."

"If you take away everybody else's pains, who takes yours?"

"Five yuan. Special."

"I don't have any pains, thank you, Grandfather." He gave the man a ten-yuan bill. As the blind man slipped it in his pocket, Tao felt warmed by his own generosity, then it struck him he could have gotten off cheaper: how could the man tell the denomination anyway?

That evening he mentioned the episode to his wife. "How come you always see dirt-poor, handicapped people in Beijing, who somehow keep going to a ripe old age?"

"My granny taught me the secret of immortality. When the man has sex with the woman, *he* should not come but have *her* come, so he absorbs her *qi*."

The briefest of pauses. "Not worth it."

Should they make the call? What alternative was there? They had to try, at least once. It was agreed that Haiping should do the talking—better it should come from a woman. Tao would listen on the extension in the bedroom. He pressed his ear to the receiver and heard the atonal music of the numbers, then the dial tone . . . What went through his head (hers too, he knew) was that surely no one would be at the other end—Liu had passed away—they were phoning the afterlife.

But an androgynous voice, gruff and breathless, answered. "*Wei. Wei.* Who's there?"

Haiping's high-pitched telephone voice: "Excuse me, we're trying to get in touch with a Mrs. Liu."

A pause—and once again Tao felt sure he could predict the response: *She died ten years ago.* But instead the person at the other end was saying, "You want to speak to her? She's a little deaf, so she doesn't normally come to the phone."

"And you are—?"

"I'm her niece, Cao Lan."

Tao cut in, explaining succinctly about the discovered cache.

"Valuable?" said the niece.

Tao replied, "Worth something," at the same time as Haiping said, "Of sentimental value."

"I thank you for bringing your gift."

The Songs had been planning a quiet evening. (Their routine on Mondays was to order in pizza and watch their favorite Korean soap opera.) But best to get it over with. She wrapped the tin in paper left over from New Year's, with a good-luck

Year of the Rat pattern. They got in their VW, Tao at the wheel. They turned onto the Fourth Ring Road and headed east.

It was farther than they'd expected ("Heavens!" said Haiping, "We're practically in Mongolia!") and they became a little lost. They kept stopping to ask directions: first from a police officer, then a woman who looked like a prostitute, then a fellow in a denim jacket who turned out to be a waiter at a Sichuan restaurant (Tao spoke to him at length in their native dialect. "What did he tell you?" said Haiping. Tao said, "Oh, he didn't know the way. We were just chatting"), then a taxi driver and a gaggle of punk teenagers, and finally they pulled into a characterless street, alongside an apartment building not all that different from their own.

Soon they were inside. A burrow of a place, subdivided by yellowing partitions. Cao—a tired, middle-aged woman still wearing the uniform from her job in a department store—padded about in plastic slippers. She marched down a corridor barking, "Auntie! Auntie!" (the Songs looked at each other and grinned tensely) and came back escorting an old woman by the arm as if arresting her; she seated her in a rust-colored armchair. Liu was not wearing her teeth, and a hearing aid was clamped to her ear like a parasite. Was there a family resemblance to the figures in the photographs? A nostalgic whiff drifted across from her; she smelled like the Songs' apartment.

The couple bowed their heads. The wife presented the gift-wrapped tin. Her husband was the ambassador; loud and slow, as to a foreigner: "We believe you hid this many years ago—"

"—when you were young," Haiping chimed in, realizing only as the words came out of her mouth that the old woman, absurd as it might seem, actually *had* been young: roughly the same age then as she and her husband were now.

"—inside your apartment, ours now—"

"—in order to conceal your bourgeois origin."

"We are happy to give it back."

Haiping peeled off the layers of paper and opened the lid, revealing the glittering hoard. She tilted it so the light caught it—some element blazed like the pearl under a dragon's neck.

For seconds Liu did not respond at all, as if she were video-conferencing from another continent. Then the vision seeped into her brain: her shoulders and knees shook, her hands flapped as if shoving away a viscous substance. Her jaw dropped—dark gums and prehistoric tongue; a bottomless gulf. The voice seemed to come from elsewhere than her body.

Shrieking, "No! Not mine! I never saw it before in my life!"

Husband and wife begged, "We humbly urge you to accept . . ." "Dear Grandmother . . ." Meanwhile Cao stared scornfully at these bright, optimistic youngsters.

Liu remained in a world of her own, bolt upright now, babbling, "I deny everything! All my ancestors were proletarians!" She sang a snatch of "I Love Chairman Mao More Than My Own Mother and Father," her voice soaring ear-shatteringly on the ultimate high note.

Cao cleared her throat like a machine gun. She hauled her aunt from the chair and led her, still singing and muttering, away. The niece turned from the waist to glare at the visitors: "You two had better leave."

Back home, the Songs considered their options. Surely the cache did belong to Liu, but if she disowned it . . . He said, "I guess we'll just have to mail it to her." She had to agree; she volunteered to do it.

Tuesday she was in her office. The tin was on her work desk, next to a mock-up of a pop-up children's book about an animal sports tournament, for which she was on the design team. She murmured to herself the Olympic slogan, "One World, One Dream." Cardboard box and packaging material. She ran her fingers over the items she was bidding farewell to. None of them worth much—with one exception. She was an aficionado of a TV show about antiques, and she was pretty sure the jade spoon was Qing. She balanced it on her palm. Its bowl

was carved with a rebus of bats and peaches—a wedding gift, no doubt. The jade was pure and smooth, unscratched, as if it had been created this morning. Definitely worth hundreds; a thousand yuan most likely. And it's not as if Old Liu really wanted it, in fact she'd denied it was hers. She bubble-wrapped the spoon, till all that could be seen of it was a green gleam, and sealed it with a lick of transparent tape. She dropped it in the pocket of her computer bag. The rest of the stuff she mailed off.

Three days later, the postal service returned the package to the senders. Included was a letter from Cao: "My aunt has asked me to write . . . The photographs and postcard are not those of our family. Furthermore we never possessed a foreign book or anything musical or artistic, or a valuable compass, or spoon, or pair of glasses . . . I thank you for your trouble." The box arrived while they were having breakfast.

Tao read the letter out loud, and nodded into his rice porridge. "I guess that settles it."

"Let me see," said Haiping, reading the letter over again for herself. "Oh dear, oh dear." She couldn't keep this from her husband. "She's dropping a hint. You see, the jade spoon was *not* in the tin."

"What do you mean?"

She confessed.

"Oh, Haiping! How could you?"

"I'm sorry. I'm a bad girl." She blushed and hung her head.

"You're the best bad girl I know."

"I'm a snake demon and an ox monster."

"Thou shalt kowtow to the Emperor!"

Wearing her aqua bathrobe, she performed the traditional ritual of obeisance. Her right sleeve brushed her left arm from the shoulder to the fingers, then her left sleeve brushed her right arm. She bent one knee on the carpet, and she bowed low with her right hand at her back and her left hand hitting the floor.

"We'll send it back again, spoon included," he said. "This time, *I'll* do it."

"Whatever you command, Your Imperial Highness."

"My aunt requested I return the gift once again. She assures you that our family never possessed a tin containing a book and music and photographs and glasses and a compass and jade and a hundred yuan . . ."

The next Monday, the package was back on their dinner table. "What's all that about?" Haiping said.

"Beats me."

"You did send her the jade spoon, didn't you?"

"You know I did."

"And the 'hundred yuan'? Explain that. You didn't slip some money in the tin, did you, Tao?"

"Of, course not." He scratched his head. "Heavens! The old capitalist! Don't you see? She's implying we stole money from her, on top of everything else! And now she wants us to give it back!"

"Out of the question!"

"Oh, I don't know."

"She's a con man . . . No, it was probably Cao's scheme."

"They're both poor. We're always saying how we'd like to do something to help the old folk, those left behind by modernization. This is our opportunity. 'From each according to his ability . . .'"

"As my granny used to say, 'Don't add legs to the snake after you've finished drawing it.'"

"It's no big deal. We'd spend a hundred on a good night out. But it's a fortune for Liu and Cao."

He opened his wallet, drew out a hundred-yuan bill, and tucked it inside the tin, next to the postcard.

"That won't do, Tao."

"Why not? It's not a crime to give charity."

"I mean, we can't put modern money in there, if it's supposed to have been hidden since the Cultural Revolution. If we *must* do it, we should use old money."

"What does it matter? *We* know there was originally no money in the tin, and *she* knows, so who are we kidding?"

"We have to save her face, all the same."

He said, "Did they even *have* a hundred-yuan bill back then?"

They pondered this matter—the idea of a world that existed before they were born.

"China invented paper money," she concluded. "We have had it for thousands of years."

Tao got on the Internet and found a store in Chaoyang that sold period currency—one hundred one-yuan bills from 1969 for only 260 yuan. He offered to zip down there before work, then he'd mail that damn tin.

Solemnly she linked her pinkie with his. "We should do this together."

And so they did—the two of them stuffed the wad of creased dirty currency in the tin. How many people had cared for those rectangles of printed paper in their time, folding them inside pockets and wallets, hiding them under mattresses, sewing them into the lining of their clothing, exchanging them for what they needed or thought they needed. For a third time the treasure left them.

They waited, but it never came back. Days passed, and by the following Monday they accepted its loss. Relief combined with a dull disappointment. Let the mad old woman and her greedy niece do what they want with it. That night, after television, they brushed their teeth and went to bed early. A hand snaked out and turned off the light. In near silence, gravely, they made love. They arranged themselves with her body nestled inside the curve of his, and together they fell asleep.

They woke and made love and worked and slept, and woke and made love and worked and slept . . . And Sunday at dawn the phone rang. Moving as one, they turned over in their shared dream, not arriving at consciousness. When finally they struggled out of bed, a message was on the answering machine. They had to play it twice to take it in. Cao's voice: "*I regret to inform you Liu Kangmei passed away. She was in a coma for almost two weeks, so her passing came as a blessed relief. The funeral will take place this afternoon. Her relatives and friends and members of her work unit are invited.*"

Naturally they had no intention of attending—they scarcely knew the woman. But Haiping phoned and left a message of condolence on Cao's answering machine. Then she said defensively, "I don't know why we should be upset. She was old. She was crazy. She was in pain."

"Yes, but that kind of woman, clinging on. Somehow you think she's never going to die."

They were naked on their bed, sitting back to back.

Tao mused, "At least Liu got the tin."

"Unless she was already in a coma when it arrived."

"Well, we'll never know."

"There's only one way to find out."

He dialed. The phone rang and rang . . . He tried again from his cell phone. This time eventually the call was answered. She heard him say, "Yes . . . It's me . . . My heartfelt condolences. Now about that box we mailed you . . . No, just ten days ago . . . Really? . . . Is that so? . . . You're sure? . . . Of course . . . As I said, my wife and I offer you our sincerest sympathy on your tragic loss, Mrs. Cao. Good-bye."

Tao rocked his head back and told his wife, with an air of triumphant defeat, "It never even arrived!"

"What?"

"Cao swears they never received it."

"The old liar!"

"Why would she lie? What would be in it for her? No, I expect the package got lost in the mail. It happens all the time."

"You're positive you sent it off?" A whiff of distrust between them.

"We went to the post office together, Haiping. Remember?"

Being highly educated as well as passionate people, they analyzed their own emotions. "Why should we feel a sense of loss?" Tao said. "End of game—the score is nil–nil. We didn't want to keep it, and we haven't got it. Liu can't miss it now. The only one who's losing out is Cao, and who cares about her? And if some thievish postal workers are hawking the stuff at a flea market, that's not our problem."

"You're missing the point, Tao. The old woman didn't know we meant well. We did our best for her, in the end. We tried to give her everything she was asking for. She died thinking we'd stolen her treasure."

He echoed her, "She thinks it's still in this apartment."

Haiping stood up. Tao tipped and lay with his head on the pillow, staring upside down at his wife and the switched-off ceiling lamp.

She said, "When my granny passed away, we confused the ghost so it wouldn't come back. We changed things, to make it no longer recognize its old home."

"You mean, you redecorated?"

"Not even that. We just moved stuff around. We put the sewing machine in the bathroom, for instance."

"And did it work?"

"Her ghost never did return."

"Well," said Tao. "We were planning to reorganize our place anyway."

They seized the excuse to make some of the changes they'd been putting off for months. Still naked, they moved the carpet from the west side to the east side of the living room. They carried the bookcase in the bedroom to beneath the window in the L-shaped living room. The couch and armchair were rotated ninety degrees, and the television went with them. They shunted the bed so its foot no longer faced the door, for better feng shui, and they exchanged the blue bedspread for the green. The floor lamp from the storage closet they carried into the bathroom, and the table lamp they'd been using there went into her study. The Mao clock above the toilet moved in with the floral arrangement on the sideboard, displacing the bowl of apples, which lost its fruit (she bit into an overripe Jonathan) and became a bowl for business cards by the main entrance. They rehung Picasso's *Guernica* that he'd bought for his dorm room in college, and the watercolor of a sunset she'd made when she was twelve. And in front of the semi-ironic shrine in her study where she put photographs of her ancestors and lit incense when she remembered they placed a golden screen. She tidied up the kitchen. He changed the screensaver on his desktop. She slipped on her robe and got a screwdriver and went out into the corridor and removed the 23 from the apartment door—because those who know where they live, know, and those who are invited will be told, and those who neither know nor are invited really have no business here.

Finally they stood on their bed, clutching each other, bouncing and shouting repeatedly, "*No! Not mine! I never saw it before in my life!*" until they fell, body across body, exhausted, aching, groaning, gasping for breath.

THE THREE LIVES OF LITTLE YU

A MARRIED COUPLE without an heir, what are they but living ghosts? They had tried for five years already without success. So they decided to buy a child. A boy would be beyond their means, but a girl—in those years, in that district of Hebei Province, people were practically giving them away. They handed over ration coupons worth five jin of rice to a woman in a nearby village, and in return they received a daughter, a few days old, skinny and coughing. In heaven transparent doors opened a crack, and closed. New Year, 1959—Year of the Earth Pig. The adoptive mother had inherited an amulet from her own mother, a disk of jade carved with a lotus flower, and she tied it with a red ribbon around the girl's neck. They named her Yu, which means "jade."

They took her home. They swaddled her in the traditional manner, winding a cloth around torso and neck, wrapping her so she could scarcely move. They laid her between them on the raised brick sleeping platform. The quilt was spread over the entire family. Zheng blew softly on the baby's eyelids and she sneezed at him. Miao held the tiny sucking mouth to her nipple. Miraculously, milk began to flow.

The parents cared for her as best they could, skimping on their own rations during the bad harvest years that followed. Yu was always tiny for her age (the head oversized relative to the body) and never in good health. All the same she was affectionate, and smart too. By the time she was three she could write her own name. One day (her parents hoped), unlike them she would be literate; she would make her own way.

The girl's favorite game was Traveling the World. She walked and leaped from platform bed to chair to dresser, circling the interior; the rule was never to touch the floor. The final stage of her journey, from hope chest to bed, this she could not accomplish on her own: she always needed her parents to hold her arms and swing her across.

In the winter of that year her breathing became labored. She spat blood. The family went into debt to pay the herbalist, who prescribed ephedra to direct the *qi* downward, and *ma huang tang* to balance her yin, but poor Yu struggled for breath. One bright morning the parents awoke to discover the child motionless and cold.

The father unknotted the amulet and the mother pressed it between her breasts. They missed their daughter terribly. Their consolation was that such a good girl would surely have a happier reincarnation. *You can only go halfway into the darkest forest; then you are coming out the other side.* They buried the corpse in the field behind their home.

✳

BY 1965 THEY HAD SAVED enough for another child. But none were for sale on their own commune. They went by horse cart to the nearby town, and asked around the market. Prices had gone up; they haggled and paid two hundred yuan plus fifty jin of rice coupons. This daughter of theirs was a fine, strapping girl, a few months old. She bawled vigorously when they fastened the amulet about her neck. She bawled even louder when they tried to swaddle her, and they decided it wasn't necessary in her case. Zheng pressed his nose against hers, "Kiss your daddy, Little Yu." Miao gave her the breast, and once again milk flowed from the mother into the child.

This version of Yu was vigorous and grew fast. She was naughty sometimes, making a game of throwing her toys down, and once she broke a plate; they forgave her everything. She had a lovely smile—her mother's smile, Zheng liked to say, looking fondly at his wife; and Miao pointed out how the girl strutted with her chin up like her father. She was as smart as the first Yu; when she was six she could write a hundred characters and read twice as many. At her parents' request, she set down her name in the copybook next to the name Yu had written in 1962.

Some tattletale with a grudge made it known that before the Liberation, Miao's uncle had leased out land to poorer peasants; the family was tainted. The parents had to undergo self-criticism sessions—they wore dunce caps and a placard around the neck, I AM AN OX MONSTER AND A SNAKE DEMON—before being, some months later, rehabilitated. They took pains to demonstrate their enthusiasm for the Party. Zheng volunteered to put in extra hours spraying pesticide, and Miao babysat for other families. Yu got into a fight at school with a boy who accused her of being a capitalist, and she beat him. There was a poster above their bed showing cheerful workers at an airplane factory, with the slogan "Our Lives Are Sweeter Than Honey."

In the summer of 1973 Yu asked her mother, "Where do babies come from?" Miao laughed, and told her the legend of the Monkey King, who burst from a stone.

That autumn Yu caught measles and three days later she was dead again. *You cannot prevent the birds of sorrow from flying over your head, but you can prevent them from building nests in your hair.* The commune arranged for the body to be cremated.

✻

IT TOOK THEM YEARS to pay off their debt, working long hours in the sorghum and tobacco fields. But by the 1980s they began to think again about being parents. They were into their forties; the clock was ticking. In the summer of 1984 they made their way to the orphanage in the provincial capital, Shijiazhuang. It was a squat concrete building, from the outside like a factory but inside cheerful enough and brightly lit. No sign of children in the reception area though, as if this place dealt with the idea, rather than the fact, of orphans.

A woman in a white uniform greeted them.

Miao said, "We're here about a baby."

"It's a girl," Zheng specified.

The woman (a nurse, they guessed; maybe even a doctor) smiled sympathetically. "Oh, there's nothing to be nervous about. We get quite a lot of people like you. Leave her with us, and you won't have to worry about her ever again."

Miao stammered, "It's not like you think—"

"It's for the best, you know. We'll take her off your hands. Would you like a cup of tea?"

"Comrade," Zheng said, "it's the other way around."

"We want to adopt a baby."

Now the woman looked stern. "Oh, that's hardly likely. There's a long process applicants go through."

Zheng said, "How much?"

"Thirty thousand yuan."

The would-be parents stared at each other. The sum was fabulous, utterly beyond their means.

"Outrageous!" Zheng said. "You take babies free of charge, but you sell them for thirty thousand!"

"This is the official policy. It has been approved at the highest level."

"Please help me, Elder Sister," Miao pleaded.

"As Chairman Deng so aptly put it, 'It does not matter whether the cat is a black cat or a white cat. What matters is whether it can hunt mice.'"

At the bus station they were approached by a young man with a bird perched on his shoulder. "I'm a Buddhist monk, though I'm not allowed to wear my robe. Do you want my crossbill to tell you your fortune?"

"Our bus is leaving in fifteen minutes," said Miao.

"It won't take long," said the monk.

"All right," said Zheng. He paid one yuan.

The bird tweeted at them.

The monk had a plastic bag that contained fortune sticks. He cupped his pet in his hand, then flicked its rump with his index finger. The bird flew down and picked a stick from the bag and put it on the concrete floor, then another and another, the beginnings of a nest.

The monk looked at the sticks, studying their markings like a mah-jongg player. He asked his clients, "What do you want to know about? Money? Health? Love?"

"Yes," said Zheng.

"Will we have a baby?" said Miao.

"Oh yes," the monk said. "Definitely. This very day the baby will be conceived. The crossbill is always right."

The old bus groaned as it rose up the curving road toward the Taihang Mountains. The middle-aged couple comforted each other with traditional sayings—the distilled wisdom of generations. *You think you lost your horse? Who knows, he may bring a whole herd back to you some day . . . You cannot expect both ends of a sugar cane to be as sweet . . . A gem cannot be polished without friction, nor a man perfected without trials.* They got off at a crossroads. They hitched home on a tractor. They lay naked on the platform bed and made love.

✡

THE NEXT MONTH, Miao's period (the old ghost, as she called it) came on schedule. Her body was reliable that way. And the next month too. Not that they doubted the monk; as is well known, fortunes should be interpreted obliquely. The monk never said *they* would conceive her. Zheng and Miao concluded: given that Little Yu had been such a wonderful girl, most likely she'd been reincarnated into comfort and wealth this time. And the place to find happiness in modern China (they knew this from radio and indoctrination sessions) was no longer, as it had been for millennia, a peaceful village in the countryside. Now it was the city. And the greatest city in the world is Beijing.

They'd never been to Beijing, even though it was only three hours away. Nevertheless in the early spring of 1985 they set out. Their journey began at dawn. It was below zero, but they kept themselves warm enough, she in a quilted jacket, he in an army coat stuffed with newspaper for extra coziness and a tugged-down "old geezer" hat. They'd arranged a lift to the crossroads, where they flagged down the bus which took them to the Shijiazhuang railroad station. Their first time on a train. The express came from the far west and would terminate in the capital. They had tickets for hard seats, but found themselves in a hard-sleeper car; most of the people in it had traveled through the night, and were still dozing. Soldiers were occupying the bunks, snoring, their bare feet, smelly and innocent, sticking out over the edges. All the seats were full, containing passengers dreaming or eating soup, playing cards or gambling at the finger-counting game. So Zheng and Miao squatted in the corridor.

There were plenty of others in the corridor. It was thick with cigarette smoke. Travelers hawked and spat on the floor and strewed chicken bones. From time to time somebody would pass by, en route to the toilet or in order to fill a thermos from the hot water urn, and they'd have to stand, pressing themselves against the window. A haughty conductress clipped their tickets. A sweeper cracked a joke, "You know why they call it Year of the Pig? Because this place looks like a pig sty!" He spoke Beijing dialect, peculiar but comprehensible. (But it *wasn't* the Year of the Pig! They could only suppose he'd been making the same joke for years, as he traveled the length and breadth of China.) Another couple—the man wearing a skullcap, the woman a home-dyed indigo costume with a strange crested headdress—put a pinch of green tea in an enamel cup and poured hot water on it from their thermos. They drank from it themselves, then they offered tea to Zheng and Miao, who gratefully accepted. The two couples had no language in com-

mon, so Zheng and Miao never found out who their temporary companions were and what drew them to the capital.

Mostly they just watched. There was still patchy snow on
the higher ground, which vanished as they moved east. Wheat
fields turned into cornfields . . . soybean . . . sesame . . . a stand
of poplars . . . From time to time a group of houses would
appear, the sooty red-tiled roofs; then the countryside would
resume . . . a nodding horse . . . a waving child . . . The earth
became blacker, the air more opaque—the wheel of a coal pit.
A steel converter issued sparks . . . And twenty minutes later
the signs of industry had passed, as if it never had been. A row
of women in wide hats were hoeing a cabbage patch . . . And
now the houses and factories came more frequently. The roads
were broader and paved. A density to the air: this was a place
where things happen. They could sense they were already on
the outskirts of Greater Beijing.

In the corridor, people were walking to the toilet with a
heightened sense of purpose. Awakened sleepers were rolling
out of the lower bunks and climbing down from the middle
and upper ones—traders and soldiers, migrant workers, urban-
ites returning home, and others too who fit into no obvious
category, whose motives for travel could only be guessed at—
they might be visiting a distant relative, they might be lovers
or thieves.

Was the train nearing the heart of the city? They'd imagined some kind of wonder—they didn't know what exactly,
rainbow-fringed visions, tall lucky people bounding in giant

strides. They saw long gray blocks of buildings. Then the same thing again. *This is it,* said the wheels on the track. *This is it, this is it, this is it . . .*

Was this it? Beijing consisted, they discovered, of one gigantic brick-and-glass building. The shadow of a many-paned window fell on the marble floor. A porter explained this was merely the railroad station. "We're looking for our daughter," Miao told him, and he suggested they take the special train that goes underground.

Who would have thought of such a thing? But once you are in it, it seems obvious, natural. Badgers do it, and hedgehogs; why not humans? The line went west, back in the direction they'd come from. Eventually—"Get off!" said a conductor. "Only soldiers are permitted to remain on board. The stations beyond are for the base under the Fragrant Hills. It's built to survive nuclear war, you know."

At first this district seemed daunting, with its high, packed buildings and low, ivory-colored sky, and the dirty air made them cough. But then they realized it was like a village. It *was* a village —not so different from their own. The old women staring shamelessly at passersby, the old men on a bench carrying their caged birds, the local beauty leaning from a window and the young men ogling her while sharing one cigarette between them, the boys playing Forcing the City Gates (a single boy running full tilt into a line of others), and a girl who tossed on high a shimmering diabolo, which emitted its *wong-wong* sound. Zheng and Miao knew these people, or others much like them. When they beheld a cotton candy seller who was pedaling hard to create sweet fluff, shaping it into a sphere as big as a baby's head—though they'd never actually seen this treat before and could only dream the taste—the worn wise face of the man proved he was a peasant at heart: they could picture him picking sorghum, or sitting at the back of a commune meeting with his boots stuck out, pinching himself to stay awake.

They walked along the block, and at the corner there was a store with a glass double door that slid open automatically when people approached and slid shut afterward. They could see a dozen shoppers inside, and shelves stacked with food.

Outside was a mobile seat with four plastic wheels on its base and a metal handle on one side. An infant was strapped into the seat. She had pale skin and big eyes, and around her wrist a bangle made of jade. This was a sign. Zheng touched the juncture where the straps met, and they clicked apart. Miao crouched and extended her arms; she scooped up her daughter.

They took her on the underground train; and so to the city-within-a-city that is the central railroad station of Beijing, a multistoried palace in which at any given moment a million people are bustling to and fro, each with his or her own reason for being here, secret hopes and fears. Miao breast-fed Little Yu, and the girl was old enough already to drink a little water from a bottle cap, and Zheng chewed some cake which he spat out on his palm, and patted the pap between her pouting lips.

This third Yu was as delightful and talented as the previous versions. Her health couldn't have been better. In due course she too wrote her name in the copybook, next to the names she'd written in 1962 and 1973. She played with the cloth doll she'd had in her first life, and the building blocks she'd made a tower out of and knocked over in her second life, and at age three she was still alive, still alive at eight, and today even, still alive. She has gone south, moving to Paperclip City, where she lives in a dormitory and works in a factory with five thousand other young women; she operates a crate-sealing machine. Her coworkers are mostly natives of Guangdong Province and speak Cantonese; she's picked up enough to get by. When they ask her where she's from, she says, "Oh, somewhere near Beijing."

Though she seldom visits her elderly parents, she loves them, all the more so because they remind her who she is. She remembers her first childhood: the precious spoonfuls of sorghum gruel and how in her hunger she chewed bark off the trees. She remembers the coughing, the ache in her chest, the fever and the fading away of her body. She remembers her second childhood too: the entire school dancing the Loyalty Dance—left hand up, right hand out, *"Loyal loyal loyal / to Chairman Mao! / Boundless boundless boundless! / Forever forever forever!"*—while the commune secretary kept time, tapping a spoon on the desk. She remembers the itchiness, the thirst, the exhaustion, the pain like a hand gripping her throat. She remembers the first time she ate pizza, the first time she wore jeans, the first time a man kissed her, the first time she saw the sea.

But more than the past Yu wonders about her future. She will not be a paperclip crate sealer forever. In a few years, she thinks, when she has fifty thousand in the bank, she'll return to Hebei Province, and marry, and become a mother herself. Or else she might go to Beijing, and find herself a life there.

THOUGH THE CANDLES FLICKER RED

BLAME IT ON THE OLYMPICS. The authorities are trying to clean up the city, give it a new face. Let's fool tourists and athletes into thinking it's always been like this. Street performers of all kinds, they're swept out of sight. Not that they vanish, they relocate to the outskirts, beyond the Fifth Ring Road. Now, as I set out to work, making for the number 13 subway line, I'm importuned by calligraphers and contortionists, fortune-tellers and acrobats, and a living statue in the guise of a terra-cotta warrior poses on the traffic island. You can't just walk by these people as if they don't exist.

There's one busker who's been here since the New Year. He's staked out a spot in the underpass near the station. In his late fifties, I'd guess; gray hair and glasses; on colder days he wears a Tianjin-style ribbed jacket. Just another migrant from the provinces, I'd supposed, chancing his luck. He arranges an inflatable red cushion on the ground and sits cross-legged, the instrument balanced on his left thigh. He plays the erhu, always the same slow, mournful tune. I must have tipped him a dozen times before we finally had a conversation. "Tough out there," I said—words to that effect. It was April, dust season; the north wind blowing from beyond the Great Wall. "Not

so bad," he replied seriously, "I get bigger tips in lousy weather."
To my surprise he was addressing me in Beijing dialect—
throaty, with exaggerated tones, the way the old-timers speak.
I had some minutes to spare, and was in no hurry to go out
into the billowing dust. "How was spring in the old days?" I
asked. "More dusty? Less?" He drew the bow against the strings
and the python-skin resonator amplified the sound. I dropped
a five-yuan bill in the instrument case. Once again he performed
his tune for me, and then he told me his story.

His name was Chen Wei. His father had taught composition
at the Beijing Conservatory and his mother's father had owned
a department store; during the Cultural Revolution the family
was in Category 4, the lowest level. In 1970 Chen was sent to
be reeducated at a commune in Shanxi Province. "It was hell,"
he said. "We were supposed to 'learn from the peasants,' but
you can't learn anything when you're hungry all the time. We
could never fulfill our quotas. We intellectuals were told to
hoe the weeds, but nobody told us what was a weed and what
was a sprout."

"Did your comrades help each other?"

The bow made a discord. "Intellectuals—every man was out
to save his own skin."

"And the peasants?"

Chen snorted. "They called it the Three Togethernesses. We
were supposed to live with the peasants, and eat with them, as
well as take their advice. But let me tell you: the rule was we
had to save our shit for manuring the fields, but the peasants

kept sneaking into the latrine and stealing the intellectuals' shit."

"But you're here today . . ."

In a softer voice he said, "It wasn't all bad. My commune was in the foothills, near a bamboo forest. Shanxi is beautiful in the spring, you know . . . After a few months I moved in with an elderly peasant couple who were different. They looked after me, gave me medicine when I was sick, and made sure I had enough to eat, anyway."

He looked up expectantly. I offered him a cigarette, which he lit, cupping the flame in his palm. I put another yuan in his case, and he told me about that family.

They lived in a one-room hut, the way their ancestors had always done. They farmed wheat and cabbages and they gathered wood-ear mushrooms. Their son, Dandan, almost died during the famine years of the late fifties and early sixties. He

pulled through, and though he never grew tall he became strong. They loved him above everything and he gave meaning to their lives. But when he was older, a difficulty arose. How could husband and wife make love with the boy curled up next to them on the brick sleeping platform? In summer the couple sneaked out into the woods like young lovers. But in winter and in the rainy season, that was hardly practical. When Dandan was seven, they strung a blanket down the middle of their hut, and told their son that from then on he would have to sleep on his side of it. Even so, he could surely overhear. They found errands to send him on, telling him to collect kindling, or claiming they could hear a wild dog nearby and ordering him to shoo the flea-ridden nonexistent beast away. But it was frustrating, never knowing when the boy might come back, and always having to keep as quiet as they could, suppressing their joy.

By the time he turned ten Dandan was active and curious—beginning to be interested, the parents noticed, in girls himself. The problem was only going to get worse. The wife confided in her mother, who came up with a solution. The mother's brother played erhu; he agreed to teach Dandan. The boy, though he had no great musical talent, was persuaded to go along with the plan. Now, twice a week in the late afternoons, he sat on his side of the blanket and practiced. "Louder!" the parents would call, "Play it louder!" He only ever learned one melody, a traditional one, "Though the Candles Flicker Red," but this was sufficient. The music was jerky, out of tune, riddled with mistakes—no matter. Once more the parents enjoyed a satisfactory love life, and the child grew into a vigorous and happy adolescent.

When he was seventeen, Dandan was recruited into the army, and sent to a base near the Korean frontier. His parents were content he'd found a place in life, an honorable career. There was every prospect he'd be promoted. Who knows? One day their little boy might command a brigade. Of course the parents were lonely without him. Still, they imagined the compensation would be that they now could make love whenever they wanted, in any way they wanted, as vociferously as they dared—the entitlement of the humblest peasant as much as that of any general or lord. But to their dismay, in the absence of the plaintive music of the erhu, their lovemaking lacked a dimension.

It was the following spring that Chen arrived in their commune. At first the couple didn't know what to make of him, a comical and pathetic figure in thick glasses who couldn't tell a beet leaf from a poisonous shoot. But it was the husband, Luo, who intuited that the young man might have a hidden talent. He struck up conversation one morning when the two of them were squatting at the latrine.

"Tell me, Young Friend, I mean, Comrade, can you by any chance play an instrument?"

Chen was puzzled and guarded. Was he being tested on his bourgeois background? "What if I can?"

"I'm rather fond of music myself."

"Well, as a matter of fact I studied the cello. The piano too, of course, and I'm competent at violin and viola, and the mandolin as well."

Luo understood none of these exotic words. "Yes, Comrade, but can you play the erhu?"

Chen declared—no more than the truth—"I'm sure I can turn my hand to any instrument."

The two men pulled up their trousers, and Luo spat out his cigarette butt. "Come to my home, Young Friend, this afternoon at five. My wife would like to meet you."

Chen was welcomed. He was introduced to the wife, Shao. He was served tea and a hawberry treat. The three sat side by side on the sleeping platform, the stranger in the middle. The couple showed him the instrument left behind by Dandan. After just a few minutes of experimentation—though he'd never held an erhu in his life—he was able to produce notes on it, chords, whole melodies: "Happy Birthday," segueing into "Rely on the Helmsman While Sailing the Sea," and the opening bar of Beethoven's Fifth.

Then Shao leaned forward, her eye sockets deep and her teeth gleaming in the light from the grate. "Comrade, do you know 'Though the Candles Flicker Red'?"

"Sing it, and I'll play."

The woman hawked into the fire. In a hearty voice, a little cracked, she sang. The music filled the little hut.

Chen nodded curtly. He took up the instrument and played the tune back—richer and more shapely than they'd ever heard it before. Luo and Shao turned to one another and shared a smile.

At their age, the couple were not embarrassed to explain their dilemma, though Chen blushed. There and then, the blanket was drawn across the middle of the hut. Chen took up his position, playing the simple, wistful tune over and over again, with as much volume as he could. Meanwhile, on the other side moans and shrieks of joy.

It was agreed: Luo and Shao invited Chen to lodge with them. They would help him with extra vegetables, also herbal medicine if he needed it, and give him what advice they could. In return, every Wednesday and Saturday from six to seven the young man made music.

So Chen survived in the commune in Shanxi Province, while other exiles did not; and thirty years later he regained his Beijing residency permit. He was back now where he'd come from, getting by, using the talent he possessed.

✲

THIS IS WHAT the old man told me in the underpass during the dust storm. Others had gathered close by—a sword swallower and a man who did tricks with string, and a one-legged "want-rice" was plucking at my sleeve. I gave the musician an extra ten yuan. I could delay no longer: I had a train to catch.

"Old Chen," I said, addressing him with respect. "One last question, please. Given your experience and ability, why do you always play the same tune?"

He adjusted his instrument, settling it lower on his thigh, and gave me a sneaky smile. "Oh, there's nothing like this tune! This is the only good 'un!"—as with parted lips and half-closed eyes once again he began to play. And I had to admit, listening to the familiar melody, there was something in what he said.

THE GLAMOROUS HEART
OF COSMOPOLITAN BEIJING

YOU WOULDN'T NOTICE HER. She's skinny, hair tied back, one of those flattened peasant faces, a person of no particular age. She's in the aisle of the number 9, standing and swaying, not holding onto anything, her hands loose at her side. Yes, if you happened to be looking that way you might notice the hands; the fingers stir, making subtle adjustments; the hands are sophisticated radar systems, scanning the city on a range of frequencies.

It's midafternoon but already the bus is packed; it's the one that shuttles between Beijing Station and Beijing West Station. Migrant workers fan themselves with their big hats. An old man half-rises, groans. A monk sleeps with his mouth open. The conductor, a yin-yang medallion around his neck, whines like a mosquito, "Ticket! ticket!" A short fat woman with two shopping bags balances in the aisle.

A stop now. People are trying to get off, but the fat woman is blocking the exit. She's cursing—sounds more like she's bleating—but even if you can't understand any specific word, you can tell she's not polite. "You stupid woman, get out of my way!" a businessman in a checked suit says with a Cantonese accent. Slowly she rotates, then bangs her bag into the businessman's crotch. He yelps, stumbles. The skinny woman is close to him, her hands skim over his coat. Her face is impassive; only her hands are alive, questing—think of a parasite which must spend a portion of its life cycle inside the body of another creature. The businessman leaves the bus. Its doors close automatically. The journey continues.

The skinny woman is standing alongside a man in a brown sweatshirt. Neither looks at the other, his eyes are cold. He signals her with a lowering of his eyelids.

It's like shooting an audition reel—the skinny woman, the fat woman, and the brown-sweatshirt man, they have their given roles, but each time a different actor plays the mark. This time around, it's a woman carrying a white suitcase. Having been cursed and bumped into, and having had her jacket caressed, she too exits.

Once again the skinny woman approaches the brown sweatshirt. A minimal shake of his head. Two goes: that's the maximum per journey.

At the next stop, the skinny woman jumps off at the rear, the fat woman and the man with cold eyes exit at the front. The three of them walk over to the shade of a dumpling shop's awning and halt, as if meeting there by chance. "Dumplings?" says the man, who goes by the alias of Zhaole. He gives a ten-yuan bill to the skinny woman, Fan, who goes inside. Meanwhile Gu does her bleating at him, which he more or less understands. "Don't hassle me, woman!" There are plastic chairs and a table. Fan joins them, delivering a Styrofoam container of fried dumplings. Gu grabs a dumpling. Zhaole thumbs through the takings. The businessman's Louis Vuitton wallet contains many business cards, but less than a hundred yuan in cash. "Tightwad!" Zhaole says. There's a credit card, as well, and a Hong Kong ID, which can be fenced. Behind the ID, a photograph of a naked woman. "Cute!" Zhaole laughs. "Bet that's not his wife!" Also a promotional postcard of a restaurant: fashion models are seated on a terrace with a fountain playing beside them. Fan, who can read better than Zhaole, mouths the caption, "Take me to the glamorous heart of"— what does that character mean? oh yes—"cosmopolitan Beijing!" It's the best thing about being a pickpocket, she thinks, peeking into other people's lives. Next, the pigskin purse belonging to the white-suitcase woman, containing just a piece of paper with a penciled address on it, plus one thousand yuan. Zhaole whistles. He gives a hundred each to his coworkers, and keeps the rest for himself. He slam-dunks the wallet and purse into a garbage can.

"Are we going to do another run?" Fan asks.

"Too late," he says.

The most profitable time is rush hour, of course, but they're not allowed to work then. This is the system. Zhaole buys a time slot on a particular route from the mob that controls the Beijing buses. The mob handles the kickbacks to the conductors and drivers, and pays off the police too, though that can't be relied on. The Olympics changed the rules; the cops are under pressure from above; there's always the danger they'll arrest somebody, to make an example.

Gu is stuffing dumplings into her mouth. Zhaole says, "Hey! save some for me, greedyguts." Both aim their chopsticks at the same dumpling—it splits, pork and scallions spill out.

There's got to be three to make a team: the thief, the distracter, and the receiver. Sometimes Fan and Gu swap roles. Then Fan has to draw attention to herself (but she has little talent at that) and shove the mark. On the other hand, Gu is a natural at pickpocketing.

Fan and Zhaole have been together four years. They come from the same town in Liaoning Province. The steel mill was shuttered a decade ago; if you grew up there, you had to leave. For girls, these were the options: you became a thief, a whore, or you got a job in a factory. Fan reckons being a thief is best, though she's not ruling anything out. Or you could marry a loving, considerate, generous man, but that's just a dream. There used to be a third Northeasterner on their team, Yali, but nine months ago she disappeared, the way people do in Beijing. So Zhaole bought Gu from a gang of beggars. Gu is deaf; they say if you lose one sense, you gain extra abilities in another. She could win the Olympic gold medal for pickpocketing. She's sort of mute too, but not really. Anyhow she's originally from Yunnan—even if she spoke perfectly, you probably couldn't understand her dialect. Sometimes it crosses Fan's mind that the superfluous member of the team is Zhaole. But, well, you've got to have a man. The women sleep with him on alternate nights; when it's cold all three cuddle up together. Fan does feel jealous, but where did jealousy ever get anyone? They're family; she and Gu have shared fleas and Zhaole and bedbugs.

Besides, Gu is warm and soft, good to curl up next to. Gu has a sideline as a masseuse: she stands behind Zhaole and digs her greasy thumbs into his nape; then she practices her craft on Fan's hands, tugging the fingers hard and cracking the knuckles. Massage and pickpocketing—feeling for a wallet or for a taut muscle, they're related professions.

Zhaole looks at his watch. "We've just got time for one more go." This translates as: he's worried they haven't made enough yet. He's got expenses.

They return to the bus stop and get on the next number 9. The familiar routine. This time the mark is a white man, a backpacker in hiking shoes and shorts . . . who is suddenly yelling in fluent Mandarin, "Get your hands off me, bitch!" Fan hadn't actually taken anything yet. She tries to look innocent, hurt by the accusation. "That bitch tried to rob me!"

Fortunately they're at a stop. The whole team jumps out. They walk fast—*not* run—in different directions. Five minutes later they're at one of their rendezvous points, an intersection by a cellular telephone store. Impartially Zhaole screams at both women, "That's the way to get caught! You lose your concentration and we all end up in the slammer!" Fan says nothing. Zhaole gobbles forth profanities, the usual ones heard everywhere in China, about his mother, sister, grandmother . . . He goes, "Fuck your ancestors to the eighteenth generation!" Then he sets about punching his women, no harder than normal. It's something men feel obliged to do—so Fan thinks. He likes hitting her on the face but Gu on the breasts and belly; between the two of them, they'd make one perfect punching bag.

Soon enough this peters out. He opens a pack of Honghe and offers it around. The three of them smoke. "Well, we escaped this time," he says philosophically. Fan's face feels sore. "Am I bruised?" she asks Gu, taking care to face her so her lips can be read. Gu replies with the "not" sign—perpendicular index fingers. Zhaole opens his mouth and lets a smoke ring ascend to heaven.

It's then that Fan spots, on the ground by the phone store, a large plastic shopping bag from Three Wishes Fashion. It is plumped out symmetrically and its top is neatly bent over rather than being knotted or fastened.

As she's about to open it, Zhaole says, "Don't."

"Why not?"

"Don't you listen to the news? We're not supposed to touch strange bags. It might be a bomb."

"It's not a bomb," she says.

Gu makes a farting noise with her hand on her armpit.

He says, "Listen. Bag stealing is not our line. *The crow solves the crow's problem and I solve mine.* If we try to be somebody we're not, we'll only fuck up. We're pickpockets. People have been pickpocketing in China for thousands of years."

Fan says, "There haven't been buses for thousands of years."

"Who said anything about buses? Our ancestors had other ways of getting around. For example people used ox carts, and there used to be caravans of camels coming from the Gobi Desert to Beijing. I saw a program about it on TV."

"Our ancestors didn't pickpocket on a camel!"

"Yes we can! We can pickpocket anywhere!"

Fan unfolds the top of the bag. The bag is a darkened room and the contents glow like a movie screen. At first she's just aware of colors—crimson and sky blue, with a subdued glitter—then there's a hint of motion, a promise of change. This is fabric of some sort, cool and soft to the touch. It smells of wealth, ease, luxury. The item is folded, but it is surely a dress. Whoever wears this, she would be a star. All eyes would turn to her.

"Leave it, Fan. It's not for you," and Gu is seconding him, bleating her agreement.

But already Fan is walking away with the bag.

Fifty meters along the street there's a boarded-up warehouse with DEMOLISH whitewashed on the wall. She continues around the side, to a door that has been crowbarred open. Slips through the narrow gap. Not much inside. On the walls: graffiti—tags in Chinese; and in English, *Qingdao Punx Rule!* Ashes on the floor where a fire had been lit.

Now Gu is at the door, grunting to be let in—but there's no way she'd fit through, and probably not Zhaole either. Fan dips her arm into the bag, as if reaching into a well, and draws forth the dress. Beneath it, she realizes, are other equally wonderful garments, a whole stash of them. The one on the top is ankle-length, armless, backless—it swerves as she holds it out, it dances in the air. Perfume wafts from it, with a piquant hint of mothballs. She cannot *not* try it on!

A pleading moan behind her. Gu has entered after all—by sheer willpower she's squeezed through the crack. She is gesturing that she wants a dress too.

Fan pulls out the next one—lime-green, diaphanous—and flips it to her.

A sliver of Zhaole's face in the gap, and his voice echoes, "Five minutes! That's all I'm giving you. Five minutes to play dress-up. Then we're outta here!"

The women put on the wonderful outfits. As well as dresses, there are skirts and bodices and robes, lingerie too. Everything is made of silk and other fine fabrics; astonishing how small it all folds up—another item appears, and another . . . as if the bag is bottomless. Fan finds a pair of oxblood high heels, which she wears in place of her flip-flops.

For want of a mirror, the women swap items, each imagining how an outfit would look on herself. Fan strips off her denim and faded underthings, redressing herself completely; only her socks are unchanged, the reminder of who she is. Gu wears the stuff on top of her regular clothes. The garments conform to their contrasting body types; the materials are stretchy or pleated and magically cut to flatter them both. They pose and flaunt like models.

Zhaole's voice cuts in, an alarm clock jangling into a dream. "Hurry up! You said you'd be done by now. One more minute! That's all I'm giving you. Women! Who needs 'em? Thirty seconds! I swear, in my next life I'm coming back as a 'comrade,' y'know, a 'brokeback.'"

The grumbling voice suddenly becomes intense—"Get out, women! Run!"—overlaid with the siren of a police car. Voice and siren rise to a crescendo, then cut out.

Gu claws off her aquamarine *qipao*, a horrible ripping sound.

She scampers away—to be met by Zhaole, who has smashed a window at the back, and has come to the rescue, whether out of chivalry or self-interest. "Out the window!"

Meanwhile the sound of a key turning in the lock, the door squeaking open, a Cantonese voice saying, "I definitely saw the criminals heading this way . . . ," and it's the businessman in the checked suit, accompanied by a pair of police officers, male and female.

Zhaole hisses, "Follow me!"

He and Gu turn and run—but, entering through the very window they are aiming for, knee and elbow first, his body unfolding, it's the scowling blond backpacker, tall and ghost-pale in the dim warehouse.

"Up here!" Zhaole drags Gu after him. A ladder takes them to a higher level.

Fan is stuffing the clothes into the bag. The cops blink at the vision of the woman in the scarlet dress, and grope for their guns. She scrambles to the unlit eastern side of the warehouse. A row of bins; she dives into one (it's the big wooden kind, like those used for storing lotus roots), taking her bag with her. She pulls the lid down and lies on her side, panting.

Through a knothole, she watches the cops searching. The Hong Konger, his face a picture of fury, is making an obscene gesture. The male cop two-handedly aims his gun. Fan squeezes her eyes shut—a single shot echoes.

She waits. She half-expects to see her accomplices come fluttering to earth—two birds shot with a single bullet. But little happens. A bit of fluff drifts past the knothole.

The hunters wait it out. Eventually the white man says, "The bad guys must've climbed down the fire escape."

The Hong Konger twists his body before speaking, the way actors do in kung fu movies. "The evildoers shall not escape our vengeance!"

The two marks run out in hot pursuit.

The cops look at each other. The male says, "Those rich types, they think if they tip us, we'll catch their enemies for them."

The female says, "Hey, wasn't there a third crook, a woman? Over there somewhere?"

The cops amble across to the row of bins. Fan hears and glimpses them opening bin after bin, shining their flashlight. "Not in this one . . ." "Nope. Not this one neither . . ." Their heavy footsteps become louder. "Pickpockets are like cockroaches," the male cop opines. "You squish one, and guess what, next day there are a hundred more." The female cop agrees, "After nuclear war, all that'll be left are pickpockets and cockroaches."

Fan inhales. Just as they are about to reach her bin, she hits the lid and springs up.

She shrieks wordlessly like a fox demon.

Past the startled cops, an apparition in scarlet silk, she flounces, the bag in her arms, seemingly making for the window . . . *When the enemy thinks we will fight in the mountains, we will fight in the valleys* . . . and pivots sharply. The male cop fumbles for his gun. She weaves, heading for the shadowy northern side of the warehouse. She arrives at a loading dock, its wood rotten, a stink like rotten seaweed, and—trying not to lose her momentum, a champion triple jumper—lands jarringly on the ground below, mud and grit. She squelches out of it and jogs along the alley, still clutching the bag.

The entire block is scheduled for demolition. A brand-new shopping center will arise on this site. She is running past what was a by-the-hour hotel, and a travel agency, and a lottery ticket kiosk, and the specter of a Sichuanese restaurant. The late afternoon sun behind her lengthens her shadow, which falls on gravel and the remains of a newspaper and a broken skateboard. The shadows of the pursuing cops are almost touching her shadow.

"I bet you ten yuan I get the crook before you!" says the male.

"Done!" says the female, as she accelerates, sprinting closer to the fugitive.

How can Fan hope to evade them? Ahead: the lights and traffic of a busy road; if only she can hold off the cops till she makes it that far. Grant her a wish. She undoes her bag, and tosses a garment over her shoulder. It is a gorgeous tangerine evening gown, ruched, golden-fringed. It floats and spreads on the breeze. The female cop holds out her right arm as if stopping traffic, and barely catches the hem. The thing drifts, translucent, across her arm and face and torso. She stops to put it on, doing up the fiddly buttons.

Meanwhile the male cop is charging ahead. At his speed, he'll catch Fan in no time. Out of desperation she throws him something—a baby-blue knee-length shirtdress with a moiré shimmer and a Peter Pan collar. He makes to slap it aside; he scrunches the fabric in his fist. Then, struck by the sheer sensual beauty of it, he too slides to a halt. He fits the dress on, tugging it down over his uniform, his gun and nightstick making peculiar bulges.

Fan is exhausted, her heart beating so hard her ribs ache, the high road still in front of her like a mirage. Some power outside herself gives her the strength to keep going, staggering on her high heels. Soon the tangerine and the baby-blue cops resume their chase.

Scant seconds ahead of her pursuers, she makes it to the intersection.

A miraculous taxi is idling. She jumps in. The driver stubs out his cigarette and coughs at her incuriously. "Take me," she gasps—a second wish—"Take me to the Glamorous Heart of Cosmopolitan Beijing!"

He drives her to a district new to her. Many restaurants and boutiques, with signs in English and Korean and Japanese, foreigners and posh dogs speak into cell phones and mark their territory against the trunks of manicured trees. She scrapes her shoes on the floor of the vehicle.

The taxi pulls into the driveway of a five-star hotel.

The driver points at the meter. "That'll be thirty kuai, darling."

She has no money on her, not a single fen. What can she tell him but the truth? "I left my money in my other clothing."

To her surprise, he accepts this. "I'll see you again, darling, and you'll pay me, one way or another."

This is not the place pictured on the postcard. It is another version of heaven. The bronze doors slide open as she approaches, and a liveried doorman bows. The atrium is a bamboo glade. An artificial stream leads to a pool with real carp. A paved path takes her over a bamboo bridge and down to a seating area. A golden Buddha perpetually tickled with a laser beam presides over a bar. She takes her place on a plush crimson banquette. A waiter says, "Are you expecting someone?"

Grant this final wish—a man sits next to her. He is movie-star handsome, impeccably dressed in dove-gray suit and pointed shoes. "Let me buy you any drink you want."

What comes next? The man falls in love with her at first sight. He invites her to meet his parents. The wedding is magnificent, with a thousand guests. They reside in a villa. She wears a different dress every day. They take vacations to Hawaii and Europe. They have a son, and maybe a daughter too. The husband has a heart attack, and she becomes a wealthy and beautiful widow. Many men aspire to her hand, but she turns them all down. She makes generous donations to charity. She survives to a ripe old age, and on her deathbed she is surrounded by loving children and grandchildren. In her next life, she is wealthy from day one . . .

"Champagne?"

She's never drunk grape wine before; she likes it—fruity. But the bubbles are a surprise; they get in her nose.

The man doesn't pay the way ordinary people do; the drink is added to his tab.

He clicks open a golden cigarette case, lights two cigarettes, and gives her one. He tells her he's from Shanghai. "It's a great city, far more modern than Beijing, and a major port. Have you ever seen the ocean?"

Wishes come true, but seldom in the desired way. She has few illusions. She knows the dress may make her look more attractive and more prosperous, but it doesn't transform her into the kind of woman a man would marry. She burps, retasting the dumplings. "Lovely," she replies.

As he takes her arm, helping her up from the banquette, she notes the location of his wallet in an inside pocket. She leans against him. Her fingers twitch, scoping out the man and the bar and the hotel and the moneyed district. He leads her into an elevator which descends to an underground parking garage, and so to his Ferrari. "You match my car," he says approvingly.

His wallet is still in his pocket. She has not taken it, but she could. The city unreels in front of them. The way back is not closed, she thinks, as he drives her toward the place he has in mind.

THE UNOFFICIAL HISTORY
OF THE EMBROIDERED COUCH

THIS STORY SHOULD BE sung to a traditional tune, something slow and plaintive—perhaps "Fragrance Filling the Courtyard" or "Remembering the Maid of Qin"—accompanied by a beggar plucking the erhu. For it takes place, for the most part, some four centuries ago, during the Ming dynasty.

As with many stories from that era, it concerns the more or less tragic fate of a beautiful young woman. She is a virgin, of course, and her father has taken pains to ensure she will remain so until her wedding day. She lives in a pavilion surrounded by a garden, with a stream and a goldfish pond. She is attended by maids, and eunuchs come in to do the heavy work. But under no circumstances is she permitted to behold, or be beheld by, a normal male.

For reasons that will become apparent, I will withhold her name, referring to her under the alias of Lady Yu. Her father will be called simply the Duke. Her chief maid, in whom she confides, is of little importance, so you may as well know her real name, which is Mei. You have now been introduced to three out of the four characters who will feature in this story; I expect you have suspicions as to what kind of person the fourth will turn out to be. You will find out soon enough whether or not you have guessed correctly.

The Duke is no tyrant; he is taking the necessary precautions —so he justifies his actions. Any suitors his daughter might have, and she has plenty, are free to contact him with details of their family tree, their horoscope, and their fortune. Provided their credentials are impressive enough, he will show them a painting of her; this will only increase their ardor. They will have to wait until she is of a marriageable age; then he will choose the most suitable among them, and that will be that.

However, one day Mei (whom you recall is the maid, a flirty, simpleminded creature, but not unattractive in her rustic way) presents her mistress with a bouquet of chrysanthemums in a blue-and-white vase. "A gentleman asked me to give you this, ma'am." (Of course Mei had been paid a generous bribe for acting as a courier, but that is by the by.)

"And why would a gentleman wish to give me flowers?" Lady Yu replies, in her artless manner.

"Why do you think?" says Mei. "He wants something from you in return."

"And what might that be?"

Mei giggles. "The polite answer is, he wants your hand in marriage."

Lady Yu sniffs the flowers. "They say that gentlemen, some of them, are extremely handsome. Was that so in this case?"

"I haven't the faintest idea, ma'am. I didn't meet him personally. He gave the bouquet to a servant, who gave it to me." She giggles some more. "The servant pinched me!"

"Oh yes, I expect he is quite extraordinarily good-looking."

That night, Lady Yu is alone in her bed, the bouquet on a table at her side, when a voice begins to speak. The voice is deeper than that of any of her maids or eunuchs, though not quite as deep as her father's. "Good evening," says the voice. "Is anybody there?"

Moonlight shines through the latticed window, illuminating the fair virgin in her translucent silken gown. It seems the voice is coming from the bouquet.

"Good evening to you. It is I, Lady Yu. Please tell me who you are, and by what magic you are speaking. Did a sorcerer bewitch you and trap you within the chrysanthemums?"

"Ha," says the voice. "There is an altogether different explanation."

Can you guess what that explanation is?

To find out whether you are right or not, please continue to the next chapter.

ON THE SEVENTEENTH FLOOR of a building in the Chaoyang district of Beijing, you will find the offices of an advertising agency. Among their employees is a young man named . . . But no, I will not reveal his true name (though it is easy enough to discover, should you type the relevant keywords into a search engine). Let us call him Li. He is what they call a "creative." Specifically, he writes lingerie ads. "A delectably shimmery lightweight bra, combining traditional elegance with the latest hi-tech uplift." He yawns as he composes this kind of drivel, inserting the text beneath an image of a perfect bosom. I should add that he is heterosexual, notwithstanding.

Li is not the sort to play the field; a series of one-night stands with the kind of sluts you pick up in the bars of Wangfujing—that's not for him. It scarcely crosses his mind to seek a "little missy" at a karaoke joint, or—horrors!—a "hairdressing salon." No, Li is looking for a decent woman with old-fashioned values, a virgin, indeed, and beautiful. And where can one find such a paragon in modern Beijing?

So when he receives a spam e-mail from Heritage Matchmaking Service, he is intrigued. All he has to do is send them the not inconsiderable sum of 888 yuan (a "lucky" number) and in return they promise to find him his dream date. "Satisfaction Guaranteed or Your Money Back!"

He pays up—and that very evening he is e-mailed by the service. His date has been chosen; her contact information is supplied. He is in his cubicle at the office, working late, and no coworker is within earshot. He taps the number on his cell phone. "Good evening. Is anybody there?" he says. "My name is Li. I understand you're a single woman looking to meet a successful man. According to the profile the matchmaking service sent me, you're everything I could ask for. Hello? Hello? Please speak directly into the chrysanthemums."

"HEAVENS! SUCH A CLEVER invention!" Lady Yu exclaims, as she rummages in the heart of the bouquet and retrieves the cell phone. She has some initial difficulty in operating it; her interlocutor has to explain the most basic things, such as how to switch off the speaker phone for greater privacy. "I have led a sheltered life, and I am ignorant of the ways of the world. I can see you have a lot to teach me."

I will spare you an exhaustive account of their flirtation. They begin with matters astrological. She was born in the Year of the Monkey, he the Year of the Pig. "Monkeys and Pigs get on so well together," she says. "Remember how the Monkey King is accompanied by Pigsy on his Journey to the West?"

"And what about your blood type?" Li asks. "I'm type O. According to a magazine I read, this means I am stubborn, impulsive, and loyal. I am the universal donor, so I get on well with all other types."

"I don't think I *have* a blood type," she says. "Is this something you find out only after you're married?"

This leads on to food. Yu's absolute favorite is smells-like-fish pork served with steamed lotus roots and eight-treasure dumplings.

"Mine too!" he says. "What a coincidence!"

This is followed by a comparison of their musical tastes. She is fond of the lutelike pipa and the zithery guqin, and the erhu, of course. "My eunuchs play traditional tunes for me. What do your eunuchs play for you?"

Li switches on his iPod, so she can hear the Beach Boys and a Mongolian band called Fun In Yurts.

"Mm, catchy," she says, and she la-las along. "*Precisely* how do people dance to it?"

But before he can answer, his boss marches into the cubicle, demanding the copy on queen-sized pantyhose, due that morning. Li whispers an apology into the telephone, and promises to call back the next day.

Well, don't you think that was a decent first date? Where will the relationship go from here? Find out in the next chapter.

THE FOLLOWING AFTERNOON/evening (her time zone/his; despite the fact they are located at the same longitude, there is a difference of several hours between them; I am at a loss to explain this, and Heritage Matchmaking Service has not responded to my e-mails) they speak again.

Li tells her he's at home now. He just got back from the gym. He goes there practically every day. He jogs ten kilometers on the treadmill, and does fifteen push-ups followed by a twenty-kilo power-lift—or so he boasts. He's sweaty, and he's about to take a shower.

"My complexion is the palest. Naturally I never go out without a parasol."

"I wonder—"

"I wonder about your appearance," she says at the same time.

"There's a way we can find out," he suggests coyly.

What might the fellow be hinting at? Come leap with me headlong into the next chapter.

YES, YOU GUESSED his secret. The cell phone (the latest Nokia model) includes a camera!

She gets the hang of it. She transmits pictures of her clothing: satin shoes embroidered in gold, a pleated gauze skirt, a short-sleeved gown worn within a long-sleeved one, an "auspicious cloud" cape thrown over one shoulder, also a damask waistcoat with a scrolling peony pattern, fastened by means of that novel invention, the button. "Now you show me yours!"

And it is true he has whole rows of buttons. Soon she beholds his grinning face, a floor lamp and a New Year calendar from a life insurance company behind him. "This is my studio apartment in the upscale Chaowai neighborhood." She sees his kitchenette (a humorous picture: a banana seemed to be growing from his head), his bathroom (a clever picture: his face is reflected in the mirror), his bedroom with its unmade bed.

She reveals the interior of the pavilion: goldware for drinking rice wine, a painting depicting a monk on a mountain, *The Pleasure of Solitude.* And now she zooms into the garden.

"That's some bamboo!" he says. "What a plum tree! Love the gingko!" And, "Who's that man in the background?"

His jealousy pleases her. "That is not really a man. It is a specially trained eunuch. He is crouching next to the pond in order to write on the goldfish."

"To *what* on the *what?*"

"He is inscribing the characters for prosperity and long life. The ink is poisonous, so many of them die."

"The fish or the eunuchs?"

"The fish. To be sure, sometimes the eunuchs too. But if they live, the characters expand with them as they grow into old carp."

There follows a taut pause. "Would you like me to show you the garden, Mr. Li? Of course I'll have to get a couple of stout eunuchs to carry me in the litter, and Mei will hold the parasol."

He doesn't reply.

You know what's going through his head, don't you?

He drops a heavy, not to say crude, hint: he sends a picture of himself after the shower—naked apart from a discreetly placed clock radio. So this is what men look like, she thinks.

Finally he asks her point blank.

She hesitates.

He presses his case. "I thought we were friends, Lady Yu."

Do you think she will consent?

Gently, please, taking care not to crumple the page, turn to the next chapter.

"WE'RE TOTALLY COMPATIBLE, ma'am! He's an Ox and I'm a Rat, and his blood is type AB and he says he's sure my blood type is the same, and we have exactly the same taste in food and everything!"

"Really?" Lady Yu says, leaning back on her bed, while her toenails are worked on by her maid with a pair of golden clippers. "And does he propose to marry you?"

"Well, we haven't got 'round to that yet, ma'am. We're too busy with, you know . . . But he makes a good living, working for the service. I mean, I wouldn't be surprised if he has other girls in other places and times, but I'm the one he really loves. You know what men are like!"

"I'm not sure I *do* know, Mei."

(Lady Yu, when younger, had peeked at eunuchs, once or twice. In accordance with the surgical practice of that era, their parts had been removed, lock, stock, and barrel. When urinating, they used a silver spigot.)

"It's like this, ma'am . . ." And Mei draws a lavishly illustrated edition of *The Unofficial History of the Embroidered Couch* out from under a cushion, and she explains to her mistress what's going on, in chapter after chapter.

- Fetching the Fire from the Other Side of the Mountain
- The Hungry Horse Races to the Trough
- Snuffing the Candle
- Releasing the Butterfly in Search of Fragrance
- Letting the Bee make Honey
- Inserting the Arrow Upside Down

- The Black Dragon Penetrates the Cave
- Rolling the Pearl Curtain Bottom Side Up
- The Lost Bird Returns to the Wood

Some of these are titles of illustrations in that disgraceful book; others are the names of winning throws in the innocent game of Pitchpot that the mistress and the servant play together afterward, in which they take turns tossing a ball into a specially shaped vase.

Can you guess which is which?

THIS IS WHAT HE VIEWS. An oval face, heavily coated with white makeup, rouged and lipsticked, and the eyebrows painted on thus: ^^. The hair is stiffened with a dark viscous substance and peaked on top.

"Beautiful," he says. (Though she'd look better *au naturel*. He could have a word with her . . . but best save that till later.)

Next: a swanlike neck.

Incomparable breasts.

A Ming dynasty belly.

"A little lower," he urges her.

Will she accede to his rude request?

Heavens! the chapters are getting shorter—the relationship is developing at breakneck speed—let us hurtle to the next chapter!

"HE REALLY LIKES ME, ma'am! He gave me a sweet potato he'd roasted himself. And he showed me something he called his pipe—very pretty, made of clay, I think. He puts sweet-smelling leaves in it, and he sets it on fire. First he did it on his own, then he persuaded me to hold the pipe for him, and then he let me put my mouth on it."

"How did it taste, Mei?"

"To be honest, ma'am, it made me a little sick. But he says if I keep doing it, I won't be able to stop."

This conversation takes place while Mei is rinsing her mistress's bellyband, which is embroidered with a design of scorpions and geckos to ward off evil spirits, in a golden basin. She takes the bellyband outside the pavilion, wrings it, and hangs it up to dry. While she's about it, she also places the Nokia in the sun. (The thing is solar-powered, of course. You worked that out, didn't you? The Heritage Matchmaking Service can't violate the laws of physics.)

On the maid's return, Lady Yu passes on her latest conversation with Li.

Mei half-covers her mouth with her hand as she titters. "Well, he doesn't know what you look like down there, does he? So send him a picture of mine instead!"

The maid retrieves the cell phone. She lifts her ramie smock. The lens focuses automatically.

And when the mistress has taken enough shots, the maid suggests, "Why don't I take a picture of you too, ma'am? Just for fun, I mean. Not as if we're going to send it into the future, ha ha!"

Lady Yu smiles with her eyes. She stretches languorously on the couch . . .

Before we get too hot and bothered, let's move on.

NOW, IN OUR ABSORPTION with the amours of our heroine and of her maid, we've practically forgotten the Duke. But he's been hard at work, selecting from among the suitors, and at last he's found a man after his own heart. Well-born, rich, powerful. Furthermore he owns a vast estate bordering the Duke's own. The only negatives are that the suitor is a hunchback, and he's not young. Two wives have predeceased him, and he has no legitimate issue. But the way the Duke sees it, either the suitor will get Lady Yu pregnant, and she will give birth to a son, or

else the man will die and she'll inherit the lot. (Or—heaven forbid!—she will give birth to a daughter merely. One can but make offerings to influential gods.)

The Duke believes in doing things by the book.

He writes the name of the suitor on a slip of paper, which he places in a golden vase. He bows four times to heaven, four times to earth, four times to his ancestors—and with jade chopsticks draws the paper from the vase.

Now he pays a visit to the pavilion of his daughter.

How will Lady Yu react? Will she go along with the Duke's plan? Or will she follow her heart, and declare her passion for the twenty-first-century advertising copywriter?

All will be revealed in the next chapter.

LADY YU BOWS REVERENTLY. (Mei, silent for once, kneels in the background.)

"O Father, I humbly accept thy will."

(Well, what else *could* she do? This is no fairy tale: for a Ming dynasty lady, there is no other option.)

The wedding is set for the following spring.

With a heavy heart, she texts Li.

"LOVELY, LACY, CROTCHLESS PANTALOONS are sure to put the ooh-la-la" (he sighs, wriggles, scratches his balls) "in your tired and stale relationship. Men: buy this to show there's only one thing you want from her. Women: buy this to make him stay with you, instead of cheating on you with all the younger, prettier girls."

"Dog fart!" he curses out loud. Presses delete. Starts again.

Li can't keep his mind on his work. What's up with his girlfriend? She'd seemed so eager, but he hasn't heard from her for three days. He'd tried phoning but just got her voice mail.

It's midday. Beyond his cubicle, his coworkers are going through the motions, several are schmoozing around the water cooler. A temp in an above-the-knee skirt and nude pantyhose is leaning over the shredding machine.

His cell phone bleeps. He's got a new text.

So?

What will his response be?

(How did *you* feel when *you* last got dumped?)

Take a stiff drink, and brace yourself for the upcoming chapter.

IT IS NOW MY SAD DUTY to reveal a whole new side of Mr. Li.

Angry.

Spiteful.

Vengeful.

He'd really thought the two of them had something special. He'd invested a lot in that relationship: Heritage Matchmaking doesn't come cheap, and he had to foot the phone bill on top of that—the roaming charges alone are astronomical.

The last thing he wants is to be stuck wholly in the modern

age again—the depressing superficiality of the Beijing singles scene, the liars and phonies who haunt the online personals, the "red basket" dating events in the supermarket.

He texts right back:

> hey, ming bitch! think u can dump me, n get away with it, huh? nobody messes w li! if u dont change ur mind pronto, n tell ur dad whr he can stuff his suitor, i'll post the lot on my blog, texts n transcripts n the pics 2!!! ull be on the world wide web, bitch! amateurs of ming history n tenured professors alike, theyre gonna learn wht a shameless hussy u were!!!

And after work as he stumbles toward the subway station, wicked thoughts churning in his head, a blind busker plays the erhu, out of key with terrible loud discords, and a string snaps.

> ha ha! now u show urself in ur true colors, mr li! if u post such a calumny, *urs* is the reputation that will be blackened! no decent woman will date u ever again! as for my reputation, nobody will take the word of a commoner like urself! besides, those naughty pics were actually of mei! ps i never really liked u. i was just flirting. goodbye. lady yu.

Questions to which you will want to know the answer:

• Was Lady Yu telling the truth when she said the photographs were of her maid?

- Will Li go through with his threat, or was it just a bluff?
- Does she really like him, despite everything?
- What is the URL of his blog?

Half of the answers are to be found in the following chapter.

THE FACT IS, that shameless scoundrel, that "Li," he did indeed post an account of their relationship online—complete with lascivious details, verbatim transcripts of their most intimate moments, and a gallery of shocking revelatory images that will make your jaw drop! (Of course he did. How else would I know about the affair?) And—worst betrayal of all—he revealed Lady Yu's cell phone number.

I called her up myself, to offer my sympathies and to assure her that not every man in our era is as unprincipled and two-faced as that cad. I told her he was totally unfit to pay attentions to a caring, intelligent, sophisticated, and beautiful virgin, such as herself.

What she needs is a maturer man, who shares her interests in fashion and gardening, and has due respect for the social customs of the Ming dynasty. A man who would be only too happy to carry on a seemly, no-strings-attached relationship with a single, betrothed, or even a married lady.

We talked for almost an hour, and we exchanged photos too. We agreed to continue our conversation . . .

Further details will be revealed in my blog.

THE BEIJING OF POSSIBILITIES

SHE'S GOING TO HAVE A BABY. It's due any day now. She's a virgin, but even so.

She's twenty-nine and lives with her father, a fisherman, in a village in Hainan. She's no catch. Anyway most of the men have left to seek work elsewhere. Nevertheless.

This is how: A woman from a nearby village moved to Beijing and found a job as a shelf stacker and fell in love. She married her sweetheart, a native Beijinger; she legalized her status; she became pregnant. The two of them are living in one room—they're in no position to care for a child, but they don't want an abortion either. So here's the arrangement: The woman back in Hainan is to be the foster mother. She'll do everything a real mother does, almost, and she'll be paid an allowance as well. Maybe in five or ten years' time, the biological parents will demand the child back.

Nobody knows whether it's a boy or a girl.

In advance of the birth, she assembles a few things. A newborn-size coverlet (she buys it secondhand from a mother whose child is now a toddler). A plastic rattle with a picture of Mao on it (she'd shaken it herself when she'd been a baby). Also she knits a red acrylic baby hat and booties. Not that you need much in the way of clothing in Hainan, even in winter.

Not like in Beijing, where snow is falling.

The baby is breathing beneath the waves.

The baby is sleeping above the clouds.

The baby is curled up inside the tiniest speck of dust.

January 12. A text on her cell phone from a Beijing number. *Sorry to tell you the child passed away three hours after birth.* Then an hour later the party secretary, who has the only computer in the village, pushes an e-mail printout under her door. *Congratulations! It's a girl!*

Her father is at sea, trawling for squid. There's no one to console her. But what should she be sad about anyhow? It's not as if it was *her* baby that died. It's old news that babies do die sometimes—we are all aware of this, even as we sit at our desks or walk under the open sky, and the knowledge doesn't trouble us much. The baby had never been inside *her* body. She'd never held it, even. What has *she* lost?

A possibility. That's all. A future that will never happen.

What does snow feel like when it flutters on the skin? Like ice cream? Like dust? Like dandruff? Like cotton candy? Like water? Like steam, only hard and cold.

A year later, the party secretary knocks on her door and opens it without waiting for an answer. A kindly, middle-aged man, he and her father grew up together and had been in the same unit of the Pioneers. His eyebrows are jumping with excitement. "I've got some wonderful news for you! Remember the baby?"

How could she forget?

"Well, the baby was a Beijinger, right? And you filled out the paperwork to be the foster mother, right? So you're a Beijinger too?"

She stares blankly.

"You have a residence permit for Beijing! It took some effort on my part. I called in a few connections. We had to blur your relationship with the father—Heavens! Do you know how many people would give their eyeteeth to be a legal resident there?!"

"But I don't want—"

"Congratulations!"

She can't imagine ever leaving Hainan. The sand, the sky, the coconut palms, the sea—yes, the sea above all. The sea is always there. It's alien, unknowable, and doesn't necessarily love her, but it's *there*. The sea is her mother.

Then again, what *does* she want? How should *she* know? The man is right: thousands of people are eager to migrate to Beijing. Who's to say she isn't that kind of person?

The whole village pulls together to give her this big chance. Someone finds her a place to live, in the home of a Hainanese family in a western suburb. Someone else arranges a job for her there, at a company. Nobody's quite sure what the company does, and the salary won't be much, but it's a job! And the party secretary himself loans her the one-way fare, for bus and ferry and train.

She stands at the stop, her father at her side. He made landfall yesterday, and in a few days he'll set out again. Neither is the talkative sort; they don't look each other in the eye. Thoughts pass between them, ebbing and flowing, of parenthood and love and loss. The daughter's suitcase holds the warmest clothing she has, and one knitted bootie. The father smells as always of the ocean.

Another year, and there's a routine to her life. She sleeps on a mat on the floor of the living room of a husband and wife who are seldom at home. Her job is an hour's commute to the northeast; she works in the basement of an office building. She's on her own there, sorting the incoming mail, delivering it to offices throughout the stories above. Sometimes she's called on to make tea. Sometimes she operates the shredder machine, converting documents to illegible, off-white matter. (She's not considered reliable enough yet to be entrusted with the photocopier.) Her companions are the shredder (nicknamed by her, Gao Gao), the machine for weighing letters and the machine for franking them (twins, Bao and Zhao), and the trash can (oddly enough the only female, Xiao Bing).

The company is in the telemarketing field. The other employees, all women, wear uniforms of tan skirts and blue blouses and look down on her—the hick. *They* cold-call clients all across China. Nobody would want to listen to *her* accent. The boss is male. According to the gossip, he's in the habit of picking on telemarketers, making their lives a misery—a different target every few weeks. The victims are all pretty; this is not her fate.

The sights of Beijing? It's a gray and lonely city. Its anonymity is its consolation: you'll never again encounter the person who slips past you on the street or who sits opposite on the subway—not if you live ten thousand lives. Its vastness: so much is here that nothing is here. The stores sell things she cannot afford. If she were asked to describe in visual detail a bus or a subway car, a particular shop, a crossroads, let alone a person, she'd be unable to.

The sounds of Beijing? The couple with whom she's lodging gave her a pair of earplugs—flesh-color, waxen things, two halves of a caterpillar. "Put these in at night." She guesses the intention is to stop her from overhearing them make love, on the far side of the thin wall. She wouldn't hear them anyway. Her sleep is profound, without dreams. She wears the earplugs on her commute also. And at work too, often. Her coworkers seldom address her, and when they do it's a curt instruction or complaint. The office is located near the Fourth Ring Road. It abuts a demolition/construction site, where old buildings are being wrecked and the foundations of new ones laid. Every few days: a siren, followed a minute later by an explosion. The mail room quakes. More constantly she hears and feels the dull determination of a pile driver, the scrape and thud of backhoe and bulldozer, the tinnitus of traffic. She's within these noises, and they are within her—like a dentist setting up shop inside her mouth.

One morning in winter she feels sad, and it takes her most of the day to work out why: the date is January 12. She thinks of contacting the parents, but what would she say? *I'm sorry about the death of your . . . of our . . . Remember me? I'm fostering the little girl who doesn't exist.*

About the only excitement in her life is when the municipal security stop her. They lie in wait at the foot of the pedestrian bridge she crosses between bus and subway. In her first year and a half, it happens to her twice. She shows them her residence permit. They scrutinize it. Fake? They're disappointed to discover she's entitled to be here, and so, in a way, is she.

Who can believe in Beijing? Only those who've never been and those who've left; it comes to life in imagination and memory. The smell of Beijing? Smog. Dust. Her sinuses are affected; she has lost that sense. The taste of Beijing? She eats rice three times a day, drinks tea, not much else. The touch of Beijing? Outside boutiques, there are women (immigrants like herself, she assumes) hired to clap, to attract customers. Day and night, sun and rain and snow, the clapping goes on. Whenever she passes a professional clapper, she rams her earplugs deeper into her skull. Silent applause now: the sore palms coming together and moving apart.

The following January 12 she is called on to deliver a package—a manila envelope, padded, secured with tape—to the boardroom, which is located on the top floor. She arrives and the room is not in use. A long, shiny, oval table, many windows, a clean whiteboard and a projector. She sets the envelope on the table. She turns to leave. She becomes aware she is being watched.

The creature is inspecting her with beady eyes. It lifts a foot above the tabletop, raps its claws like a gavel on the veneer. Pigeon.

"Shoo," she says, not loud. Then she tells the bird it's making a big mistake. It should never have come here in the first place. It should leave immediately.

The pigeon ruffles its iridescent neck feathers.

In Hainan, she knew a family who kept pigeons as a hobby. Not to eat, but to race. A tiny bamboo flute was strapped to a leg of each, so that as the bird flew the flute made a whistling sound. Pigeons, they say, can find their way home from one end of China to the other.

But this one confuses itself, hovers, falls back to the table.

So far she's spoken to it in Hainanese. Now she repeats her lecture in Mandarin, as best she can.

In Hainan the most common bird is the gull. Great tribes of them mew in the harbor. Fishermen are of two minds about them. On the one hand the birds compete with people for food. On the other, they circle above shoals, directing the men to the catch.

And what do pigeons direct you to?

The thing must have been here a while; a blurt of droppings sits on the table. Its feathers are the bluish gray of the roads, and its droppings are the color of smog. She stretches a hand to pat it, and it scrabbles away across the shiny surface—a motion that is neither walking nor flying.

She pushes a catch on the window and tilts the pane on a horizontal axis. Outside, dirty snow veils the surrounding earth and machinery; the sky is a ceiling of dirty snow. Cold air rushes into the room.

"Out!"

The bird stays put.

She tries lying to it: "It's fun outside! Let's go flappity-flappity-flap all over the city!"

She tries honesty: "Listen, pigeon. You don't want to be indoors. It's boring here. Trust me. As a matter of fact, if you refuse to leave, you'll die. Sure, if you leave you'll die too, soon enough—" She blocks its retreat with her body. "Shoo!"

The pigeon muddles to the metal base of the open window. It coos at her.

She stands on tiptoe and stretches her arms to look large and threatening.

Now it sits atop the window frame. It coos some more.

"Shoo, you stupid trespasser!"

It clings to the frame and still won't leave.

She leans out, inhaling the cold, and paddles her hands at the creature, actually touching it now (the mass of it, its residual strength as it labors past her palm and wrist, aiming to return). She mimics the command of the pigeon keepers in Hainan—*Ooh! Ooh!*—and it withdraws a meter or so. She thrusts a fist through the air; momentum carries her forward. The pigeon watches her pass, then ambles once more indoors.

She flaps her thought-wings as she plummets through the crisp winter air. It occurs to her that her death will be assumed a suicide.

"Typical lack of consideration," the boss will say, "leaving us in the lurch without the customary thirty days' notice!"

"That hick had no manners," the telemarketers will say, "an unfashionable hairstyle, the wrong kind of nail varnish—now look at her!"

The couple from whom she's renting will wait a few days, then clear out her stuff and rent the mat space to someone else.

The whiteness approaches—suddenly pure, not dirty— and soon she is within it.

Somehow she's curled up, both cold and hot at the same time. The snow must have broken her fall. She's in a dune of white, not quite as high as she is tall.

She waits here. No knowing how long.

She hears voices: a gaggle of women—the telemarketers—calling her name. Normally they speak in their telephone voices, high-pitched and artificial, each aiming to sound like all the rest. But these are their real voices, more varied and true.

She squats on her heels.

One telemarketer comes so close she can see the other woman's snow-stained uniform, feel the thump of her heart. She hunkers down further.

The voice of the boss himself, declaring her name.

She waits it out. The voices fade away. She looks up at the white disk of sky.

Eventually she detects steady, plodding footsteps. A different voice, a male one, gentle—"Are you there?"—spoken with a Hainanese accent.

She stands up. "I'm just fine. How are you?"

He crouches next to her hole. He's in coveralls and a yellow hard hat. His face is illuminated evenly by the reflected light, genial wrinkles around the eyes.

"I was looking for you." He adds, "You're in the snow."

It's good to have a man state the obvious. She removes her earplugs. The rich complexity of the weather and traffic sounds, and of his voice: "Have you eaten?"—a conventional greeting.

"Oh, I'm not hungry."

"Good. Good. Do you want to come out?"

"Yes, please."

He lies prone on the snow, and her hands fit inside his, ample and gloved. He pulls on her sharply, like a trapeze artist or like a man landing a fish, and now she is above ground, winded. He sets her upright and brushes snow off her sweater and jeans. From somewhere he produces a battered metal chair—a red inventory number painted on the seat—which he erects on the snowy rubble. He invites her to sit down. Her shoelaces have come undone, and he bends on one knee to fasten them. He tells her his name, which is carried off by the wind. She whispers hers.

They talk in their mother tongue, as if they've known each other a long time. He grew up inland, a couple of hours' drive from her village, in fact. He's been in Beijing three years, working in construction; he's what they call a parallel citizen—not legal, having to pay protection money, but doing just fine. He yawns a lot: he's tired; he's been up since dawn.

She tells him the story of her life, yawning herself from time to time, all the way through to her fall.

He laughs, and she can see the funny side.

"I wonder where the pigeon is now," he says. "Probably in the mail room, doing *your* job!"

He offers to escort her back to work, but on second thought (he checks the time on his cell phone) he's got to dash. "My wife's busy, and I promised to pick up our son from school."

"Oh there's no need—"

"We're going to see a movie later. It's a cartoon about penguins. They live at the North Pole, or maybe it's the South Pole?"

"—I can go back on my own."

"Bye-bye, Miss Xu." He strides away.

At the office, the telemarketers gasp and shrink, as if they're seeing a ghost—a refugee from the Yin world. The boss himself intercepts her. He says jovially, "Come here."

He guides her into the elevator and up to his private office. In the adjacent boardroom a meeting is taking place, attended by chairs of departments from several divisions, including the boss's boss.

The boss's secretary arrives with a greenish raincoat to cover the junior employee's wet clothing. It fits well enough.

"And a dose of medicine for you, too!" the boss says, opening a filing cabinet and unscrewing the cap of a bottle of Johnnie Walker. He pours a shot into a Styrofoam cup, hands it to her, then raises his own cup. A silent clink. Together they gulp the choking liquor.

He leads her out through the boardroom, bypassing the mildly curious conferees. The windows are all shut. The table is clean of droppings. Several people are talking in English. The boss says to nobody in particular, "This is one of our most excellent and faithful employees."

He personally escorts her to the exit. "Take the rest of the day off. *Please.* You need a little peace and quiet. Don't we all?"

Instead of returning to the subway, she heads east. The street is broad and lined with expensive shops. An inflatable arch, red with golden characters, advertises a New Year's sale at a department store. She passes through.

She hears the ping of her cell phone, and even before checking she knows what the text is about. The boss is firing her. He will not risk an unstable employee who might attempt suicide again, perhaps successfully, and shame the entire division. From her first job in the city she's achieved everything she could have hoped for.

She spent centuries in that snow pit, but it's still midafternoon. The sun is bright now. Her fellow Beijingers walk along, smiling in the sunshine. The city contains every kind of person she can imagine. Gently she jostles among them. A busker plays the happiest of sad tunes on his erhu, and the sweet-potato seller has sweet potatoes for everyone. Glorious cars glide past, a flock of brilliant bicycles, buses filled with contented souls. Thousands of fascinating conversations cross each other in the chill air. How wonderful to be alive in the Beijing of possibilities.

She arrives at the grandest of intersections. Vehicles nose forward. Everyone on foot waits by the curb, as at the starting line of a race. And now the lights change. From north and south, east and west, pedestrians advance.

LOVE! DUTY! HUMANITY! VIRTUE!

THE REAL STORY began a few years after the story I'm about
to tell you. I'd been born on the commune, and knew nowhere
else. This much I understood: things were changing. But was
the change taking place in myself or in my country? Was there
acne on China's chin? Was hair sprouting in the armpits and
groin of China? Were the wet dreams unreeling in my own or
China's night?

It was in the spring of 1979 that I had the first hint of an
answer, when Uncle Ha received a letter. There was only one
person who ever wrote him: his friend Zhang. The two men
had fought side by side against the American devils in Korea,
and had been injured in a bombardment during the Battle of
the Chongchon River. Zhang didn't live so far away—a couple
of hours on the far side of the nearest town—but they seldom
met in person, keeping in touch by mail every month or so.

Uncle was seated on his special chair, his wooden leg un-
screwed and resting on a stool of its own; my job was to crouch
beside him, massaging his stump and rubbing in Hundred
Flowers Ointment. Slowly and carefully he read the letter,
passing on gossip concerning his friend's health and finances;
I scarcely listened. What I cared about was the stamps! I already

had quite a collection. (I was famous for it on the commune, making a pest of myself begging used envelopes, which I soaked in water till the stamps floated off. I had a complete set of the Centenary of Stalin's Birth, and of Study Science from Childhood, and four out of the five Thriving Trades of the People's Commune.) But these were like nothing I had ever seen. The colors were gaudy, the images jaunty. The stamps illustrated the legend of the Monkey King on his Journey to the West. On the five-fen stamp, Monkey was using his Magic Needle to defeat Princess Iron Fan. On the ten-fen, Monkey was somersaulting over clouds, 108,000 *li* at a single leap! I'd been taught these stories at school, as foreshadowings of Mao's own strategy; Monkey and Mao had both set out on a kind of Long March; both had defeated wicked enemies by a combination of determination and guile. But since when was it acceptable for stamps to be fun?

"Hmm, interesting," said Uncle, who liked to maintain an air of mystery about his dealings. "According to Corporal Zhang, certain kinds of private enterprise are now being tolerated. He has made a suggestion to me. I will write back to him this very afternoon."

I dug my knuckles into the scar tissue.

"Ah, that feels good." He shifted position on the flag-red armchair. "I think I may confide in you, Little Friend, that Corporal Zhang is prepared to offer me, at a most advantageous price, a machine that will make a special kind of candy, light as cotton wool, in the shape of a ball, which is attached to a stick. It is to be sold at a profit."

"Can I taste it, Uncle?"

"Soon everybody will taste it!"

First Uncle discussed the plan with my mother (his sister), who was in charge of our finances, and then with my grandmother, who was the moral authority in the family. Uncle mailed payment to his comrade-in-arms. Zhang had a friend in town who was keeping the machine in his storeroom. Obviously Uncle couldn't pick it up on his own, and it was harvest time so no other grown-up was free. Which left me.

I was ushered into Grandmother's room to receive her permission. The room was a windowless cavern. Photographs of her two husbands and of her parents and of Sun Yat-sen were propped on the bedside shrine, and incense sticks smoked. A picture cut out from a newspaper was attached to the wall with rice gruel: a ruined monastery, the monks carrying a placard, THE BUDDHIST SCRIPTURES CONTAIN NOTHING BUT DOG FARTS. I bowed before Grandmother. She was short, and wrinkled as a peach pit.

Mother prompted me, hissing in my ear.

"Please may I go to town to pick up the cotton candy machine, Grandmother?"

A murmured verdict. "You may, Grandson."

In her ancient presence I acted younger than I was. I made a pun ("grandson" and "monkey" are homophones). "I am the Grandson King! I see the Machine already in my Magic Mirror! I'll somersault to town over the clouds, and if any bad person tries to stop me, I'll bash him with my Magic Cudgel!"

Grandmother sighed, "Nothing but dog farts. Bear that in mind, Grandson."

"Thank you, Grandmother."

Uncle wrote the address in town on a sheet of paper, which Mother sewed into the lining of my coat for safety, along with ticket money. Old Fatty gave me a lift on the tractor to the railroad station. In a film I'd seen, a boy hero presses his ear to the track to listen for the enemy. I didn't.

This was my first train journey on my own. A jolting local, to me it was speedy. I squeezed through the crowded car and perched on the edge of a bench, acting casual. Through loudspeakers stops were announced and music crackled, "The Red Army Crosses Ten Thousand Rivers, Yearning for a Moment of Rest." In my excitement I needed the toilet. I waited in line behind farmers, soldiers, important officials, all of them smoking, and I inhaled their smoke, coughing along with the adults. The toilet was just a hole in the floor. Crossties and gravel and the occasional weed flew past. I did it as slowly as I could, leaving my mark, I reckoned, on a full kilometer of track.

As we pulled into our destination, another train parked on the opposite platform; the signs indicated it would be heading that evening to Beijing. I imagined that city as built on a mountaintop: a man could stand there, looking down on the whole of China. In the commune there were several people (the generation younger than Uncle, older than myself) who'd been Red Guards and had stories to tell of the rallies in Tiananmen; a carpenter named Chen had personally spoken to a woman who'd spoken to Zhou Enlai. But the only person I knew ac-

tually from there was Teacher Peng. He'd been sent to Shanxi Province to be reeducated, and had fallen in love with a local woman; he'd lost his Beijing residence permit and would never be allowed back. He taught art—the one subject at which I had talent. "If you work hard at your colors, Young Man, maybe one day you'll study painting in Beijing." I had two yuan in my pocket. I was alone. I was free. What was to stop me from sneaking on the train and making it all the way to the capital? What, indeed?

I ripped the stitches with my fingernails and pulled out the address paper. I showed it to a man selling tea eggs in front of the station. He squinted at it and pointed vaguely north. Then another man told me to go west. A woman feeding a baby said I should head south as far as the market. I walked half an hour, but didn't see a market, and the road ended abruptly in a brick wall. I didn't mind, in fact I liked the delay. There's a pleasure being in a place where you're a stranger: if people don't recognize you, then whatever you do, it's not *you* doing it. The town dwellers seemed sophisticated to me: they wore ankle boots or dress shoes, whereas on the commune we made do with secondhand army shoes, and here the girls my age had their hair in braids, which we'd been taught to think of as bourgeois.

A man was watching me. Skinny, balding (his bare head must be cold, I thought), a scabbed leather coat. He tossed aside a cigarette butt. "Are you lost?"

"No."

"Are you hungry?"

When he asked, I realized I was. He was eating a meat bun, and he was holding a paper bag containing, I could smell, several more.

"If you jump over that ditch, I'll give you a bun."

The ditch ran beside the road. It was slow-flowing and stank. Green slime coated the sides. There was no conceivable way any child my age could jump across it. I paced back as far as I could, sprinted forward, and—with a superhuman leap—landed splash in the middle. I flailed my arms, twisting midfall like a cat, and managed at least to land upright, keeping my head above water.

The man made no effort to help me. But he didn't laugh at me, either; I gave him credit for that.

I waded to the side and hauled myself out.

"Your prize."

The bun was on the flat of his hand, the way you feed a horse. My hands were dirty, and I thought of biting it from his palm.

Instead I wiped my fingers on my coat as best I could, grabbed the bun, and pushed it in my mouth.

He turned his back on me, and walked away.

I reached for the paper with the address on it—it was soaked through, illegible.

Now what?

A sense of loss overlaid with exhilaration. If I could not read the address, then I could not pick up the cotton candy machine. Without it, I could not return to my family. So I would have no choice but to head for Beijing. The night train would be leaving at eight o'clock. I would not return to the commune until many years had passed, and I would be rich and famous. I would seek out my aged mother and uncle and my ageless grandmother, and we would all forgive each other. I would present my mother with the largest, most splendid jar of Lotus Blossom Skin-Whitening Cream in the world (she was always lamenting her complexion) and my uncle with a surgical team to restore his leg. Grandmother would want no gift other than my existence; I was her only grandchild; she had said, "If it wasn't for you, I'd be a ghost." The four of us would jog side by side across a field of sorghum, toward the setting sun. The credits would roll, martial theme music would play, and "Based on a True Story" would hover on the screen.

The sky was overcast; I had hours to kill. I wandered, turning at intersections as the whim took me, not entirely at random. I was aiming for the cluster of taller buildings. That would be downtown, and from there I'd be able to find the station.

The sidewalks became broader and the shops larger; a bus rumbled past and a boy my age breathed on the window pane. Here was the Friendship Store, with a mysterious sign in English. A black curtain was drawn inside the window; I was reflected in the pane. A uniformed guard glanced at me.

Coming out of it were the strangest people I'd ever seen. Man and woman—I was sure of that, though both had hair down to their collars. He had a beard the color of buckwheat, and her breasts stuck out like a shelf. They were tall. They wore tan pants and shirts with many pockets, and carried several black leather bags on straps around the neck. Their sandaled feet were like the feet of peasants.

"*Ni hao?*" she said. (How are you?) The ordinary words sounded exotic in her accent.

I gave them a polite, conventional response, asking if they'd eaten already.

They didn't seem to understand. He said, "*Meiguoren*" (American)—answer to an imaginary question.

I tried to communicate by writing the characters with my right index finger on my left palm, but this didn't help.

The woman took a camera from one of her bags and aimed it at me. What did she want my picture for? I told her not to, remembering an Albanian film in which infiltrators photograph innocent people, but she'd already clicked the thing. The man patted my head.

It was an odd-looking camera, larger than most. A rectangle of plastic popped out, pale on the side facing me, which she waved as if saying good-bye or like somebody signaling with a handkerchief. She gave it to me. A faint image appeared below the surface, which deepened and gained color like stormy weather: here was a boy who was not quite a boy anymore, wearing army pants and shirt that had once belonged to a grown man and had been cut down; the coat was stained, the high-water mark halfway up the chest. I'd been photographed before, but this was different. The boy on this plastic was myself and not myself. The man shot me with a different camera, and she took out a third camera and took me with that too.

She also gave me this: a slab covered in paper and foil (she peeled it bare); the inside was darker than dried blood. She touched the piece to her own lips, then mine. Opium, was it? I'd been taught about it in history. But that was for smoking, and this was food. Sweet, with a cloying aftertaste. She smiled, and I thought maybe I could come to like this eventually.

The couple walked along the road and I followed. They entered the hotel for foreigners, and, since I was with them, the guard did not stop me. At the desk they picked up their key. They took the elevator. I climbed the stairs. I pressed my ear to their door. Sounds of objects being moved about inside, and speech in their language.

Outside the adjacent room was a pair of long shoes, polished to a shine. Over the back of a chair were a waiter's jacket and cap. The cap fit snugly on my head. I wore the oversize jacket on top of my coat. I spat on my fingers and rubbed my face, cleaning myself a little. I tried to guess what was going on inside: the rhythm of their lives. Uncle Ha never saw the American devils face-to-face. On the third day after he arrived as a volunteer in Korea, he was in a foxhole, sharing a cigarette with Zhang, and next thing they knew they were in adjacent beds in the field hospital. Zhang had an arm amputated. Uncle Ha reckoned the two of them were lucky. "You're bound to lose something in war." Once Uncle Ha showed me a piece of paper that the Americans had dropped over the Chinese lines. A packet of identical ones had tumbled from a plane; the paper was soft, and the soldiers kept them for use in the latrine. Uncle had a piece in his pocket when he was evacuated. "Save your life! Lay down your arms! Walk slowly toward the United Nations lines, waving a white cloth!" The paper urged them to shout, "Love! Duty! Humanity! Virtue!"—and they would not be harmed. It only now occurred to me to wonder why Uncle had kept the paper all these years. I picked up the shoes and knocked.

The man opened the door. Both he and the woman were wearing robes (his green, hers blue) that made me think of a film set during the dying days of the Qing dynasty. I hadn't expected their recostuming, along with my own; the next feature had begun.

"Your shoes, Comrade," I said, putting the pair in his arms. Politely enough, he gave the shoes back.

I tried to give them to her, but she wouldn't hold her hands out, and the pair dropped thudding on the floor, right side up but not parallel, the feet of an invisible man doing a dance step. The Americans looked puzzled and mildly annoyed; it was obvious they didn't recognize me. For them, I was just another confusing, confused person in a nation where the unexpected is sure to happen. To the end of my days I would remember their appearance, and they'd forgotten mine so quickly!

I backed out.

The door was opened, the shoes were flung out, and the door closed again.

I waited a few minutes.

I heard the sound of the shower being turned on.

One more minute.

I entered. The bedroom was empty. The door to the bathroom was shut; water noises and human noises. This was my chance. I pulled open the dresser drawers.

And there it was, on the top level. A stash of photographs. Not in an album, just loose. Hundreds and hundreds of them. Some of buildings or scenery, but mostly of people. All kinds— infants to elders, rural to urban. People from near here and others from elsewhere in Shanxi, and still others who must live in distant parts of China. The foreigners had picked the people out according to some system of their own. What did they plan to do with us? In the Albanian film, the enemy spies made themselves up to look like patriotic peasants. Was there a place in America where they'd create doubles of all of us? Would some American be altered surgically and dressed to resemble me? I didn't believe this, but what was the alternative? That my likeness would be sold; all of ours would be.

I tugged at the drawers below. In the very bottom one I found a briefcase. The hissing of the shower ceased. I opened the briefcase and shoved the photographs inside.

The bathroom door swung, and the man came out, then the woman. They were naked and damp. Hair on them in places where it shouldn't be, and no hair in places where it should.

He was shouting. She, too—a high gasping yelp.

They ran toward me, their wet feet slithering on the linoleum floor.

I dashed out, and down the stairs, through the lobby . . . *The Monkey King kept a magic needle in his ear. He expanded it till it was as long as a city, and vaulted away from his enemies* . . . They were grown-ups, and I was only a child, and there was no doubt in my mind they could have caught me—certainly they would have—if only the contents of that briefcase had meant more to them than the shame of running naked through a hotel in a foreign country.

It was dark now, on the streets. A half moon overheard.

"How do you get to Beijing?" I asked an old man carrying a caged bird. "I mean, where's the station?"

I asked the way of other passersby, and kept running till I was out of breath, and then I walked.

I walked past houses and inside families were eating supper, a child seated between his mother and his father.

I walked past alleys where women in skimpy clothing stood on the street, calling to men; and I was old enough to understand what this meant.

I crossed a bridge over a canal. The road was dim here. All I had to go by was the moon.

A racking cough. "What's going on, boy?" It was that man in the leather coat again.

I said nothing.

"I gave you a bun," he said. "Now you have to give me something in return." This wasn't fair or logical. I'd jumped into the ditch at his request. But then grown-ups, in my experience, were seldom fair or logical. He stared at the briefcase: "What have you got in there?"

"Pictures."

"Dirty pictures?"

"Just pictures."

"You collect things, do you?"

"I collect stamps . . . and other things."

"Me too." A muscle in his forehead twitched.

He took the briefcase from me and opened it. He looked at the photographs and stirred the puddle of faces. He seemed disappointed. He reached beneath, and found a pocket, which he unzipped. He whistled. It was a bundle of paper, bound with a rubber band. Maybe a score of identical rectangles, not pretty, white and black and green, the number 100, some words in the Americans' language, around the face of an elderly long-haired white man (or woman). "Hmm. Not worth much to you. Pity they're all duplicates," he said. And in case I didn't get it, "I'm taking this."

I said, "Can I have just one, as a souvenir."

He sucked through his bad teeth. "No." He added a word of advice, "Don't trust anybody. And don't believe anything anybody ever tells you—including this."

I was no fool. I knew he was stealing a fortune that might have been mine. And I knew that, as men go, this man was a weakling. But for all that, he was stronger than myself. If I tried to argue or fight, I'd just lose face. At least I had nothing further to fear from him; of all the ways men exploit men, theft is the most innocent. I spoke the words that had fallen from the sky onto Uncle—"Love! Duty! Humanity! Virtue!"—understanding that these syllables—"*Aì zé rén dé*"—must have some other meaning in English, and having a fair idea what this must be.

He replied, "*From each according to his ability, to each according to his need.* What do you need, Comrade?"

I thought about this. I thought about all the things I needed, and the things I wasn't sure whether I needed. Beijing. The whores on the street. The breasts of the white woman. A father feeding rice to his son . . . I said sadly, "The one thing I need, it's a cotton candy machine."

"Wait here." He disappeared into the night.

I waited. I buttoned up the stolen uniform, and I hugged the picture-filled briefcase close against my chest. I imagined the Beijing-bound train on the platform, the passengers getting on board, the official blowing his whistle. I remembered a legend Grandmother had told me: *The Monkey King boasted he could travel anywhere. Buddha dared him to prove it. So the Monkey King voyaged as far as he could, till he arrived at the very edge of the world. There he was at last, standing on a plain, with five mighty pillars before him. He gazed heavenward: Buddha's face was smiling down at him. And the Monkey King realized he'd gone no farther than the palm of Buddha's hand.*

Just as I was about to give up came a clamor of clanking, dragged metal, accompanied by the familiar cough. The man had been as good as his word. The machine consisted of a metal bowl with a spindle, attached to a framework. He showed me where the propane cylinder would fit, and how the apparatus should be linked to a bicycle, so when you pedal the bicycle, the bowl rotates. He explained the practical mystery of it: you pour ordinary sugar in, and it turns into a magical substance.

The man lit another cigarette and gave me a puff. Then, between the two of us, we transported the machine to the station. He got me as far as the platform where the train would arrive that would take me to my commune. He spat bloody phlegm on the tracks. Once again he turned his back on me, without farewell.

Uncle and I assembled the machine. It required two people to operate it; I did the pedaling while he was in charge of the propane burner. He also dipped the chopstick in the spinning fluff, creating the miracle, lightweight and round as the world, which, when put between the lips, is warm as a quilt and sweet as sleep, and dissolves into nothing.

I dropped out of school to help Uncle. We had a good business, which became more profitable as years went by. At first we made only the plain, white variety; but then we obtained a special powder which, when added to the candy, gives it color and taste. We offered red-bean flavor, and cola, and even peach.

RISE UPWARD TO THE BLUE CLOUDS

IT WAS NO ONE'S FAULT. She grew up in a village in Liaoning Province, and when she was little her father's brother went away to America; five months later, in a city named Detroit, he died of a burst appendix. Since he had not paid off his loan to the snakeheads, the debt now fell on her father. He loved her, but he had no choice. She stayed with her parents and her two brothers until she was fifteen. Then she had her first period (*the old ghost*, her mother called it) and it was time for her to leave. She was taken to Beijing, where she would be living with a more prosperous family (the husband was originally from Liaoning), working as their maid. She would receive board and lodging; her wages would be used to pay off the debt plus interest. It was calculated that in another twenty-two years nobody would owe anyone anything; she would be free.

She was not unhappy. She'd dreamed of a villa like the ones in the movies—chandelier and swimming pool, butler and liveried chauffeur—but her new home proved to be an apartment in a high-rise in the Haidian district, luxurious compared to the hut she'd grown up in, but ordinary enough by urban standards. She was the only servant. The family consisted of a businessman in his forties, a short fellow with glasses who was forever yelling into the telephone (something to do with export of electronics) but quiet enough otherwise, and his wife, a tall, well-dressed woman, a few years younger. The wife was in charge of the household, issuing commands concerning the proper use of dusters and brushes and patent cleaning products. The work was tolerable. The maid took a certain satisfaction in getting down on her knees and scrubbing the tiles on the bathroom floor till they were squeaky clean; it felt good to tidy up, putting every little item back where it belonged. The loneliness she could cope with.

She'd heard horror stories, about girls sent to the big city to become "maids" who are forced into prostitution. Also of servants who are forced to live in filth and eat garbage. By comparison, she should be grateful. She had a small room of her own—a closet, really—next to the kitchen. Her uniform was comfortable enough, if not flattering. Her food was adequate— ramen noodles for breakfast, and for supper rice with some kind of leftovers. What was there to complain about? Sometimes Mr. Duan stood too close, and breathed heavily. Once she forgot to lock the door of the bathroom while showering; he walked in "by accident," stared a few seconds, muttered "Excuse me," and backed out. She knew she wasn't pretty—hardly any hips or breasts, acne on her chin; no man would lust after her seriously, especially not a man like Mr. Duan, who could afford a mistress. As for his wife, Mrs. Tian, she was severe within limits. The toilet paper was being replaced: the roll slipped from the maid's fingers and fell in the bowl—a complete waste. Mrs. Tian pinched her cruelly on the knuckles.

Another time she was in the living room dusting the bowl of fruit (cantaloupe, mangosteen, starfruit, kiwi) and she could not resist a peach, the most commonplace among all these exotic specimens. She polished it against her sleeve and patted the fuzzy skin caressingly against her lips. She bit in, not realizing her every move was reflected in the feng shui mirror above the doorway. A hiss of "Thief!" and Mrs. Tian was slapping her open-palmed on the fruit-filled cheek. The maid swallowed, "I'm sorry, ma'am. I'll never do it again." The slap didn't hurt much, really; Mrs. Tian was careful not to damage her. And the peach was nothing like as tasty as those that grow in the orchards on the terraced hillsides of Liaoning Province.

Would she survive to thirty-seven? And then what? She couldn't imagine reaching that age, or having a career or marriage of her own. Not in this life. But provided she was virtuous and filial, next time around she'd be born wealthy. There is a saying of Mao's she'd been taught in school: *We are like the frog at the bottom of the well, who thinks the sky is only as big as the top of the well.*

Her education and companionship came from TV. She studied the soap operas—many of which featured rich people and their maids. Quite often the rich people would be wicked and come to a bad end, while the sassy maids would find true love; she understood this is nothing like real life. The reality shows likewise. She was a fan of *Supergirls*: a humble daughter of peasants, her hair in the latest cropped fashion, belts out a pop song; the viewers phone in their votes. "Here is your check and your recording contract"—nothing will be the same for the winner again. The slogan was *If you want to sing, sing!*—but the maid, though she crooned "Though the Candles Flicker Red" to herself as she cleaned the apartment, knew she had no voice at all. On her favorite show, *Collector's World*, a panel of experts travels to some far-flung corner of China, and local people bring in their antiques. (Reassuringly, the same scenario every week, with minor variations.) Here is a celadon bowl with a decoration of good-luck bats—nothing special to look at. An old man says he inherited it from his great-grandfather; during the Cultural Revolution he saved it by burying it in a pigsty. The experts tell him, "This vase was once in the Imperial Palace. It is worth a hundred thousand yuan!" The old man and his wife cry for joy. Then another man shows off a vase, almost as tall as he is, painted in many colors and gilt. He says it has been in his family for twenty generations. The experts examine it; they declare it is a modern forgery; an expert strikes the vase with an iron bar, shattering it into ten thousand pieces.

She'd arrived in winter, at the beginning of the Year of the Pig, and by spring she scarcely noticed the smog anymore. When seasonal gales came from the north, bringing choking clouds of yellow dust into the capital, she told herself this was the soil from her province, from the hills and the plains, the orchards and the steel factories, from the latrine behind her family house and from the yard in front of it where she'd practiced diabolo tricks till she could do "A Wild Goose Lands on the Flat Beach" and "The Golden Cicada Casts Off Its Shell" and even—flexing the string to make the disk leap a meter or more into the air—"Rise Upward to the Blue Clouds."

She tied a cloth over her nose and mouth, and continued dusting the way she'd been told, for all that the dust kept blowing back in.

There were things she knew, though no one had ever told her. Mr. Duan was not Mrs. Tian's first husband. She had a daughter from her first marriage. How old was the daughter? Where was she now? In the apartment there was one room, locked, which the maid was forbidden to enter. She deduced this must be the daughter's room. She amused herself with fantasies. The daughter had died of some horrid disease and the room had been kept untouched ever since she'd passed away. Or—better—the mummified corpse of the girl was laid out on the bed. Or the daughter was a cripple, a retard, a scarcely human mutant, caged within the room, and in the dead of night the parents would creep out and turn the big key in the lock, to feed mush to their beloved freak and scoop up her mess. She smiled as she poured disinfectant in the lavatory; a tap on the button and the thing flushes.

She found the truth out in May. Mr. Duan and Mrs. Tian invited another married couple, Mr. Qin and Mrs. Fang, over for drinks. The maid eavesdropped as she served bowls of Japanese snacks and delivered a jug of mango juice and a bottle of whiskey. Mrs. Tian and Mrs. Fang had known each other in high school in Tianjin, and they giggled as they reminisced in their local accent.

Meanwhile Mr. Qin asked Mr. Duan, "Where's little Fenfen now?" The maid paused with the tray in her hands.

Mr. Duan replied, "Oh, Sufen's quite a big girl these days.

We sent her to boarding school in England. It costs a pretty packet, I can tell you."

Mrs. Tian emphasized, "She is getting a broad-based education."

The tray wobbled and a shot glass fell off. With brush and pan the maid swept up the shards.

The parents did not seem ashamed of having exiled their daughter; on the contrary, they were taking pride in it. Was the girl being punished? Or was this how modern Beijing families operate: the father in Beijing, the mother on the moon, and the child in her own orbit? During the winters in Liaoning, the entire family—parents and brothers and herself—had slept side by side: a cozy huddle on the heated brick sleeping platform.

In the kitchen, Mrs. Tian twisted the maid's ear. "Stand *still* when waiting to serve. No wonder you're always dropping things. Jumpity, jumpity, jumpity! In your next life you'll be a flea."

The maid looked at the reflection of her ear in a silver teapot—an interesting shade of red. She wouldn't mind being a flea—bite everybody, and go from bed to bed.

In the living room Mrs. Fang was saying, ". . . has such a quaint northeastern accent, where did you find her?"

Mr. Duan said, "We had her sent from the countryside."

Mrs. Tian said, "She's a treasure. And not too expensive either."

Mr. Qin agreed. "Yes, you have to get 'em fresh from the countryside, before they come to Beijing and they're spoiled."

The maid entered with a tray of red-bean cakes, which she set down on the table—and without any visible embarrassment the others switched their conversation to the forthcoming Olympics. "I'll bet you a million yuan we're going to dominate the medal table!" Mr. Qin said patriotically.

"Our athletes are the best!" said Mrs. Tian.

The maid had never known how much her employees appreciated her. Later, as she tidied up, she popped a left-behind cake in her mouth, and in her confusion she used the spray cleaner with the blue label on the veneered table when she was supposed to use the one with the red label. She wiped the surface down with a paper towel. No harm done.

A month later the daughter appeared, a tall girl who resembled her mother but with paler skin, who gestured and strode like the foreign star of a dubbed film.

"Hey, you're the new maid," she said, the very morning of arrival, holding her hand out almost as if they were equals. The two of them were about the same age.

"*Hello,*" the maid said in English, shaking hands experimentally, gently squeezing the tips of the girl's fingers, and she blushed.

"My name's Sufen, but my friends call me Phyllis. Who are you?"

"I'm Wang," the maid said. "I mean, I'm the maid. I'm Ningning—that's my milk-name. My real personal name's just Ning."

"That's a silly name," Sufen said. "You should be called Anita, like any normal person."

"*Good-bye*," the maid said, exhausting her knowledge of English.

"*Gu bai*," Sufen mimicked the maid's pronunciation, and giggled. "Hey, do you want to know something, Anita? *You* think it's time for breakfast, but according to *my* internal clock it's about three in the morning. I'm going to stay up all night!"

"Internal clock?" said Ning. "What is this? Please show me."

"Do you have a boyfriend?"

"Of course not!"

"Me neither. Turtle egg! I'm in boarding school, it's like being in prison. You can see my pictures."

Sufen took a camera from her handbag, and operated the controls. "This is Sussex."

Green field in the foreground; behind it, an old building of red brick.

"Ah, *Sussex*," Ning said.

Then: the same building with a door open, and in the doorway a white girl with yellow hair in a purple uniform.

"This is Delia."

"Ah, *Delia*."

A lawn at a slant angle. Several more girls waving at the camera, or ignoring it. A group shot of perhaps a dozen girls, one of them Sufen, the others of varied races though mostly white, carrying long curved sticks.

"This is hockey. Field hockey."

"Ah, *hockey.*" Ning wondered who had held the camera for that shot.

More pictures of the game—including one of a fat brown girl waving her stick ferociously ("Parvati's a demon at hockey!") and of a girl flat on her face, her skirt rucked up, in front of the goal. "We lost that game. Turtle egg!"

And finally a small room with three narrow beds in it—that did indeed resemble a jail cell, or a hospital ward—two white girls in underwear with uniformed Sufen in the middle, their arms linked. "Me in my dorm. Suzie and Ginny are such losers, but we love each other." Ning looked carefully; hard to tell from the expressions of the roommates if they were happy or sad, and Sufen too was inscrutable.

"Is Sussex a good place?"

"School is hell!"

Then Mrs. Tian walked along the corridor, and the maid pretended to be dusting a baseboard. When she'd gone by, Sufen said admiringly, "You're so skinny, Anita. Are you on a diet?"

"No."

Sufen lifted her T-shirt and pinched her own slender waist. "Do you think I'm chubby? Go on, tell me I'm an elephant."

The maid pursed her lips.

"You're my thinspiration, Anita!"

"Elder Sister, there must've been a maid here before me. What happened to her?"

"Ha ha! You'll find out."

The daughter yawned and went into her room, where she lay fully clothed on top of the quilt and fell asleep.

The door was ajar. Ning studied the body. Such white skin. She guessed that's what happens when you live in England: your skin becomes whiter, and your hair becomes golden, and your nose grows, and a fold appears in your eyelids.

Then the maid went to the bathroom. It was her time of the month, and she had her usual cramps. Nothing to be done about it, really.

Thereafter Sufen was never as friendly as on the first day. She was busy, for one thing, always on the phone, chattering away with her friends in Mandarin or Beijing dialect or what must have been English, and she went out often, staying up till all hours. Ning wondered if she'd failed some test. A comment she should have made on seeing the pictures, perhaps? A week after their first conversation, when she was cleaning the girl's room, she emptied the basket, which contained a used tampon—a foreign brand with a red flower on the packet. And when she entered the bathroom to clean it, almost at noon, there was Sufen, only just gotten up. Her hair wet from the shower, she was naked apart from a long green towel draped over her shoulders, and the string of a fresh tampon was dangling from her. She was brushing her teeth, spitting a white foam into the basin. She saw Ning's face reflected in the mirror, and she stuck out her tongue at her.

Ning continued to observe her, and she could tell she was being observed in turn. Sufen seemed to eat nothing except fruit, and Ning could swear she once heard the girl vomiting in the toilet. In July, when Ning had her period again, she noticed that Sufen was having hers—one less tampon in the package. Did the daughter realize the two of them were now synchronized?

At the beginning of August, Sufen went away on a weekend trip to the beach at Qingdao with her stepfather, and when she returned she was sullen. "Turtle egg! I'm going back to school at the end of the month."

One afternoon Ning was alone in the apartment. She was on the couch in the living room, operating the remote—a weepy soap opera, a nature program about migrating birds, a classical concert in aid of earthquake survivors, a Hong Kong movie featuring shadowless ghosts, a commercial for a face cream that will take years off your age—when two pale hands swooped over her eyes, and then she could see nothing. "Ha ha! You didn't know I was here, did you?"

"Let go, Elder Sister!"

"Call me Phyllis."

"I hate you, Phyllis!"

"Thank you." The girl released her grip, and she was grinning. "Now I want *you* to help *me*."

"No, I can't."

"It's for school. I've got to write an essay, 'What I Did During My Summer Holidays,' but of course I can't tell them what I *really* did. Ha ha! So instead I'll write about you."

"Me? There's nothing to say about me."

"There's tons to say about you! You're a star! If you came to my school, the girls would ask you a zillion questions!"

The maid blushed. The daughter sat down next to her.

"Like, for instance, let's begin with the basics. How many hours do you work?"

"I work all the time. I mean, I work whenever your mother tells me to work."

"How much do you get paid?"

"Nothing." She tried to explain the story of her uncle, but she wasn't sure Sufen understood.

Anyway the girl cut in: "Is Mummy mean to you?"

"Oh, not really . . ." (wondering how much was safe to reveal) ". . . a bit, sometimes."

Sufen asked more questions, and coaxed out of her that Mrs. Tian had hit her on a number of occasions. She seemed fascinated by this. "Did it hurt? Did it hurt a lot?"

Ning averted her gaze.

Sufen asked, "And what about Daddy?"

"Oh, Mr. Duan never hits me."

"No, I meant . . . you know." The daughter's eyes gleamed. "Men are beasts!"

And Ning found herself confiding how the man ogled her; how he would pass in the corridor and in the kitchen, pressing closer than he needed.

Sufen bit her lower lip and nodded slowly during this account. "They have only one thing on their minds." Suddenly she pounced —jumped on the maid and tickled her under the armpits. "I caught you, Anita! I caught you this time!" And what went through Ning's head as she writhed and gasped and begged for mercy was that Sufen was behaving like a girl half her age, and she wondered if Sufen would ever grow up.

Sufen vanished. It happened a week before she was supposed to return to boarding school. The previous evening she'd come in late, grunted at her parents, ignored the maid, and went into her room. In the morning her parents assumed she was asleep. Eventually her mother knocked on the door, and it swung open—displaying the absence of the daughter. The bed was unslept in. Mr. Duan asked the maid, "Did *you* see her?" She lowered her head. Nobody explained anything further to Ning; she pieced together the events from overhearing the rounds of frantic phone calls. The only rational explanation was that the girl had let herself out during the night—though she hadn't taken so much as her phone or credit card. It didn't seem possible she'd been abducted, given there was no noise or sign of struggle, and besides she must have turned off the burglar alarm from within the apartment. The alarm was a clue.

Two days later, the parents, carrying one suitcase each, left the apartment. Mrs. Tian declared, "We'll be away a little while." Mr. Duan said, "We're going to London—" while simultaneously Mrs. Tian mouthed at him, *"Tell her we'll be in Shanghai."*

It was strange yet familiar being in the apartment on her own. By force of habit, she cleaned the place from top to bottom every morning. She reckoned there was enough food in the freezer and pantry to keep her for a couple of weeks. She ate little, rationing what she had. The one thing she did not touch was the bowl of fruit in the living room—though the dragon-fruit turned soft and brown, and the apricots shriveled, and fruit flies danced over the entire bowl. If the Duans still did not return, she'd have to sell an ornament of theirs at the flea market in order to get by, say a porcelain statuette or a scroll with calligraphy.

Mostly she just watched television. A week later, she happened to be flipping through channels when her attention was caught by a well-groomed man orating in a solemn voice. A current affairs program: "The Problem of Indentured Servants in Today's China." Apparently families go into debt, and as a result men and women are forced to labor in pitiful conditions, for little or no pay, for years—sometimes their entire life. Ning sat up on the couch. The television was talking about *her*. She was excited and embarrassed, as if a spotlight were aimed at her forehead. The program contained footage secretly shot in a brickyard and in a clothing factory. The camera cut to a dank alley, where a reporter was about to interview a real indentured servant: "She made a brave escape from the ordinary-seeming

Beijing apartment where she was forced to work as a maid."
The camera panned to reveal a skinny girl in filthy clothing,
streaks of dirt on her cheeks. She spoke in a Liaoning accent,
crying as she related how she'd been a slave practically, how
her mistress beat her, how her master treated her as a sex toy.

Ning switched the sound off. The television ghost continued to gesture and weep, the lips moved, though nothing more
needed to be heard. Ning knew something no other viewer
would know—even the journalists for all their skillful ques-
tioning would not have found this out—that in three days' time
the runaway would be bleeding between her legs. *Now that Sufen
has become Ning, what is left for me to be?*

She unlocked the daughter's room and shut the door behind
her. There were framed photographs on the dresser showing
the girl in the uniform of a foreign school; a younger version
squinting at the camera, a red kerchief around the neck; and a
female infant held up between Mrs. Tian (a beauty then) and
some strange man.

She glanced in the drawers. She found a notebook filled with
tiny English writing; a pink flower was pressed between the
pages. She opened the closet, patted the clothes on the hangers—
enough for a whole dormitory of girls—and sniffed. She
crouched, looking under the bed: dustballs there, which a good
maid should have cleaned up instead of sweeping out of sight.
Also a hockey stick; it was bulkier, somehow more three-
dimensional than she'd imagined, tape wound around the
handle the better to grip the thing firmly with both hands and
smash it down.

Let nothing be gripped, nothing smashed.

The young woman, whoever she was, sat on the bed. She stretched face-up on the red silk coverlet, legs together, arms at her sides. Her eyes were open. She remained as still as she could.

THE DOUBLE-HAPPINESS
BALL BEARING FACTORY

"STILL PLAYING PING-PONG?"

"Haven't held a paddle in years."

"Me neither."

"You're looking high and mighty, Huang. What are you up to these days?"

"Oh, this and that. Here and there. I work at a joint venture, the local end of a South African mining company. I guess you could call me their fixer. Our offices are in Shanghai, I'm just back in town for a meeting . . . And yourself, TJ? You must be in college. Beijing University, I take it?"

"Where else? I'm a junior now."

"Well, fancy that! Our Little Brother, TJ, is already a junior! Another year, and they'll kick you out into the real world. Any idea what you'll be doing then?"

"Not as such, Huang."

"Well, if you're looking for a connection . . ."

"I hadn't really thought about mining."

"Oh, mining is not the point. Now listen, TJ, I got my job through a, well, they're a headhunting firm. They specialize in linking people like us with foreign companies. With your language skills and your background, you're a shoo-in. Allow me . . ."

The younger man, Li Tianjun (known as TJ), in jeans and sweatshirt, bowed slightly as he received a business card from the older man, dapper and cosmopolitan in an Armani suit. The meeting was taking place in a seafood restaurant by the Houhai Lake in Beijing. There was that air of wonder at the mysterious workings of the universe revealed that one always feels whenever one chances on an old acquaintance. TJ was on his way to the terrace where the birthday party of a dorm mate was in progress. Huang was coming back from the men's room. They'd known each other at high school, where, though several years apart, they'd been on the same team.

Huang had written the name of the headhunter on the back of the card, and TJ examined it. "I guess you'll be earning a commission from Steiner Zhao Associates, should they take me on?"

"That is a consideration, Little Brother."

"I could still whip your ass at Ping-Pong, Huang."

"I wouldn't be so sure of that."

There and then, facing each other across an unoccupied but not yet bussed table piled high with soiled napkins, glassware, silverware, chopsticks, cracked lobster shells, and the remains of dishes made from oyster, sea cucumber, abalone, shark fins . . . , the men mimed the game.

TJ served, tossing the imaginary ball a good thirty centimeters in the air, and smashed it across with his signature reverse pendulum backspin. Huang smiled and chopped. TJ performed a textbook example of a power loop, forcing the ball low with just enough topspin to bring it down on the enemy side, un-returnable. But Huang *did* return it, his dream paddle almost vertical, reflecting the attack back. TJ held his own imaginary paddle at forty-five degrees, cavalierly waited for the ball to bounce high, then whipped it hard. With brilliant side-to-side footwork on Huang's part, he switched from defense to offense, deep-slicing the ball. This game could go on forever.

Except that it couldn't. "Let's call it a draw," Huang said, walking across and shaking his opponent's hand.

"*No worries, mate.*" TJ replied in English.

Ping-Pong had been the one activity in which TJ had excelled at an early age; he'd been something of a prodigy at it, in fact. His coach—a tough veteran who'd personally beaten the best Nixon's America could offer—had urged TJ to concentrate on this talent of his, reminding him of the game's importance to the nation. "If it wasn't for Ping-Pong, we'd still be in a bear hug with the Soviet Union." But TJ spent tenth grade as an exchange student in Melbourne, and came home with a fondness for Vegemite and milky brown tea, and an awareness that he could present himself to foreigners any way he wished. He dropped sports and did just enough school-work to get into Beijing University. It was there that he had social contact for the first time with those less fortunate than himself: strivers from distant provinces mumbling nonidio-matic Mandarin, in many cases the children of peasants, whose lives were set to become scarcely comprehensible to their parents.

TJ joined his friends, who were playing a raucous dice-guessing drinking game. He noted Huang at the far end of the terrace seated opposite a woman in a scarlet dress. She did not look like a business contact; but that was no concern of his.

The following morning, hung over, he rolled out of bed and checked his e-mail. He'd been tracked down. A message from Steiner Zhao, suggesting he contact them to arrange an appointment. He made himself a cup of tea and nibbled a Ritz cracker. He phoned their number.

The office was on the tenth floor of a modern building in the Chaoyang district. The interviewer, Mr. Nie, greeted him in English. *"I'm ABC myself, American Born Chinese, y'know, and I gotta tell ya, I envy guys like you, born into it. You know things we outsiders can never know."* But once he switched to Mandarin he came across as bland and detached; his was the accentless voice of a civil servant, a spokesman. "Mr. Huang told us all about you, and naturally we have conducted our own investigations." He glanced at the résumé. "You attended the elite High School 101, and you are now majoring in international relations at PKU. That's fine. Your English is fluent. Any other languages? *Deutsch? Nihonga?*"

TJ shook his head.

"That is no problem. English is always sufficient. Now, more to the point. We understand your father is a high-ranking cadre. Your maternal uncle is a general in the army. And your great-grandfather traveled with Mao on the Long March. We couldn't wish for a better background."

TJ said modestly in English, "*Oh, don't mention it,*" and translated himself into the equivalent Chinese idiom, "Where? Where?"

The interviewer leaned forward. "At Steiner Zhao, we consider ourselves to be the contemporary equivalent of old-fashioned matchmakers. On the one hand, we represent foreign companies —no doubt with experience in their own field, but lacking local connections. On the other hand, those such as yourself."

TJ said, "I don't have any particular knowledge of business or industry."

The interviewer flapped his hand dismissively. "That is not important. You understand *China*" (stressing the English name of the country—an exotic land of wonders and opportunity). "You can advise foreigners whom to speak to, how to behave, when the right strategy is to show anger, and when it's best to be patient, you can tell them" (switching languages briefly, as if avoiding an eavesdropper) "*who to pay a private commission to, and how much.* And most important of all, you have connections."

TJ nodded. "Where do we go from here?"

"Leave it with us, Mr. Li. There's no hurry; it's a year till you graduate. We'll match you with the perfect partner." The interviewer leaned back in his swivel chair. He lit a Marlboro Red and pressed one on TJ, who, though he was in the process of quitting, felt obliged to accept. The men were wreathed by celebratory smoke. Then, smirking, to the tune of Mendelsohn's Wedding March, Mr. Nie sang, "*Here comes the bride / Big, fat, and wide / Pull down her panties / And see what's inside!*"

And TJ dutifully laughed along with the representative of Steiner Zhao Associates.

The company was as good as its word. TJ sent them his transcript, photographs of himself in costumes of varying degrees of formality, his family tree, and his horoscope. In return they acted vigorously on his behalf, and in September TJ signed a letter of agreement with a Brazilian firm interested in pork. The salary was excellent. They had bold plans to establish a vertically integrated hog farm, slaughterhouse, and meat products manufacturing plant in Anhui Province. "We'll sell every part of the pig, except for the squeal." However, in October the Brazilians canceled their invitation to have him visit their headquarters in São Paulo, and the news came through that their parent company had gone bankrupt. The Anhui hog project would remain a dream.

TJ was not too concerned. He'd find another match.

As it turned out, a month later he was offered an even higher salary, with stock options, by a Vancouver-based financial services company, which would be providing personalized investment advice to high-net-worth individuals. TJ was impressed and enchanted—the topic seemed up his alley, and he felt confident he'd get on well with Canadians. He smiled inwardly every time he saw a tourist with a maple leaf on a backpack, or came across some reference to North America, or to snow. He listened to Leonard Cohen songs on his iPod, and read pages i to xiv of the preface to the *Cambridge History of Canada*. But this match too failed. Steiner Zhao hired a private detective, and discovered that the CEO of the Vancouver company had a record of convictions for fraud.

So then, a lucky escape. Good thing he hadn't signed on the dotted line. He had a nightmare in which a posse of Mounties chased him down on the campus of Beijing University.

His third serious offer came appropriately on the fifth day of the new year, when it is the custom to honor the God of Wealth. The company was from Taiwan. Generic pharmaceuticals. Unlike the others, their business plan was more mature: they already had a factory in Chongqing. They paid him in advance too, and in cash—US$10,000 in return for a promise to consider no other partner for the next three months. But the very next day TJ was in calculus class when he got a text from Mr. Nie. He stepped out and phoned back immediately.

"What's up?"

"Bad news, I'm afraid. The Taiwanese company, their founder was born in the Year of the Horse, and you, well, you're a Rat."

"So? I'm a Capricorn too, for what difference it makes."

"Ah, as the saying goes, *The Rat steals the fodder in the Horse's stable.* They have a strict policy of never hiring Rats."

"But surely they knew from the beginning?"

"Somehow there was a mix-up. They thought you were an Ox."

"I was born a week before New Year's."

"Exactly."

Silence on the line. Then Mr. Nie said in English, "*Hey, you made 10K for a one-night stand!*" He cleared his throat. "There are several possible partners for you, Mr. Li. We'll get onto it right away."

Instead of returning to the lecture hall, TJ went to the library and looked up traditional Chinese matchmaking customs. He found a volume, *Love and Courtship in the Tang Dynasty*. Not much had changed in the millennium since. Love was not the point; marriage was a matter of commercial considerations. And which role was he in this relationship? Was he the innocent virgin seeking a generous and powerful protector? Or vice versa?—as he preferred to fancy. He read a legend of a girl whose father took pains she should never go out into the world. But one day she wandered through a gap in the wall before her father found her. "What is that creature with fluffy hair that goes *baa*?" "It is a sheep, my daughter." "And what is that creature with big dangly things that goes *moo*?" "It is a cow, my daughter." "And what is that tall, two-legged, bearded, thrillingly handsome creature that is staring at me?" "It is a tiger, my daughter. If you go close, it will devour you." And the girl replied, "I have a strange longing to be devoured."

A month later Steiner Zhao proposed a match between TJ and a Swedish manufacturer of specialized steel products. A medium-sized but ambitious concern, seeking a toehold on the mainland. Given his previous disappointments, TJ did not raise his hopes too high. The Swedes sent a representative— a Mr. Peterson—to vet him. The men met at the Arizona in Wangfujing. TJ had prepared for an in-depth interview, but as it turned out Mr. Peterson seemed content to lean on the bar.

"I'm not here to judge your professional qualifications—I'll leave that to the experts at Steiner Zhao. I'm just here, well, to make sure you look and sound okay."

"And do I?" TJ wondered what the Swedes had feared he might be.

Mr. Peterson licked salt off the rim of his margarita and sipped. "It'll work out just fine."

So it did. TJ graduated in May, and immediately began acting as an intermediary for the company, helping them find connections and get permits—a task he found intricate and challenging and curiously satisfying. Initially they imported Scandinavian steel into China; but after just a year they got permission to launch a joint venture (an achievement for which his own contribution was essential, so TJ prided himself), and work promptly began on constructing and equipping the ball bearing factory in western Shandong Province. Less than a year after that, the plant was operational.

His salary was raised. He was promoted twice. He was appointed to the board of the local subsidiary, as it expanded its business on the mainland.

Five years after joining the company, he finally made it to Stockholm, where he was introduced to the CEO, Nils "Bill" Hekkema. Who confided: "Remember when Steiner Zhao got us together? Well, they sent their fellow over to check us out— some man from Hong Kong who didn't speak any Swedish and actually didn't know much about the steel business. Now at that time we didn't even have a factory up and running—we were just starting out, you know. So we got him in a car, and we drove him past a factory belonging to a rival company! We told him it was ours! And he went back and reported we were legitimate."

"All's well that ends well, Bill."

"Indeed, TJ."

Years have gone by, and TJ continues doing what he does best. He remains faithful to the company, and the company is faithful to him. He is thinking of settling down, but it is more convenient to keep a mistress, changing her for another every so often. He does not play Ping-Pong—except in his dreams (a series of powerful serves; he mixes his returns, now driving, now looping, now pushing, now chopping; the opponent never knows what to expect. He mounts the podium, "The Olympic Gold Medal for Table Tennis is awarded to Li Tianjun of the

People's Republic of China"—"March of the Volunteers" blasts from the speakers, the stadium brims with applause). Instead he has taken up golf, for business reasons and on the recommendation of his cardiologist.

His mother has passed away, and his father, like a sage of old, has retired to the countryside—a cottage near the Great Wall—where he plays the erhu and calligraphs poetry. A devout Communist throughout TJ's childhood, now he has become religious, a regular at the local Buddhist temple. When TJ comes to visit, he too lights an incense stick at the shrine in the living room, in front of the framed photographs of his mother, his grandparents, and his great-grandparents.

He wonders. His parents stayed together, but did they love each other? And the ancestors before them? How did they all meet? Through matchmakers, presumably. And what other possible mates did they consider before arriving at the chosen one? There must be tales of proposals, of counterproposals, of tough negotiations, of betrayals, of deceptions, of compromise, of missed opportunities, the final pairings to some degree arbitrary. Yet had not these matches been made (TJ thinks, as he bows and wafts the aromatic smoke), then his grandparents would never have existed, nor his parents, nor himself, nor the binational Double-Happiness Ball Bearing Factory in Shandong Province.

SANTO DOMINGO

THERE IS MORE TO LIFE than work, or so they say. Consider a man named Bao, who for the last twenty-three years has been an exemplary employee of As-You-Wish Dynamo, located in the Fengtai district of Beijing. The company makes specialized products, mostly for export—if somebody in Canada needs a component of an electric bicycle, or a German concern is manufacturing wheelchairs, or the Japanese have invented a lift that takes the elderly in and out of their bathtub, they turn to As-You-Wish, and the order will be shipped promptly, and at a competitive price too. Bao's job is to operate the machine that wraps wire around the armature. He works eleven hours a day, six days a week. What with the forty-five-minute commute on top of that, he sees little of his wife (she's a ticket inspector on the subway) and even less of their son, Tingting, who is now seven. When Bao sets out in the morning the boy is asleep, and the boy is in bed again by the time the father returns at night. So the family is together only on Sundays. They've been to the zoo and the circus, they've done kite-flying and ice-skating in season, but usually they like to sit around at home, all three of them pretty worn out, chatting. "What's new at school?" "What's been happening in the subway?" "Let me tell you something funny somebody did at the factory." To please his son, Bao makes up stories about heroes and villains, wizards and dragons, who live in faraway lands. Also there are the public holidays, but then they visit his wife's parents (his own are dead) in Daxing. This region is famous for its watermelons, so every summer they are obligated to carry the largest, heaviest, most perfect-looking fruit all the way home. Bao is not unhappy to get back to work again.

It's May 2008 and, in honor of the forthcoming Olympics, Bao is not getting time off on Labor Day. The logic is unclear, but it's what the management decided and he's in no position to argue. (Anyway he can use the overtime pay. His son demands a certain pencil that all the other boys have, and he insists on eating the Captain brand of instant noodles; Bao has to provide.) But then, to his surprise, that very afternoon his boss stops by the armature-wrapping machine and tells Bao he is to meet with the boss's boss.

This man is in his twenties and wears a suit. His teeth are snaggled, though; Bao concentrates on the teeth. A shaking of hands.

"Hello, Bao Aimin. Now, I understand you're one of our oldest employees."

When I began working here, you were a boy not even as big as Tingting. "Yes."

"And times are changing. We've all got to be more flexible."

When I was your age, I belonged to a work unit. It was our whole life. "Yes."

The man sucks in his lower lip, and Bao knows where this conversation is going. He's about to be fired. He'll never see As-You-Wish again! To calm himself, he visualizes the man as an overgrown child, and then as a wizened ancient.

But instead: "We're switching you to the night shift."

"What?"

"Just for three weeks. There's a fellow there who had appendicitis, so you'll be covering for him."

"I don't understand."

Now the man gets a little angry. "Bao Aimin, what's there to understand? You'll be doing the exact same job you've done for donkey's years, only on a different schedule. Standard pay. As soon as the other fellow is back on his feet, you return to day shift. Got it? Oh, and we're giving you tomorrow off, unpaid, so you can get some sleep."

"What?"

"*Sleep. Dreams,*" the man explains, as to an idiot. He mimes it, tilting his head, and he briefly shuts his own eyes.

"Ah, yes."

"You've just got to switch your internal clock. It's like when I went on my honeymoon to Hawaii."

That's it. Bao leaves the office. And in the evening he repeats the conversation for his wife's benefit, the two of them sharing the precious insight into the lives of the more fortunate (*Hawaii!*), and the following morning he is still at home while Tingting is eating his rice porridge.

"Hello, Daddy. Why are you here?"

Bao tells him. The boy goes to his room and comes back with the globe. "See! Here it is! Right in the middle of the Pacific Ocean!" Then Tingting explains about "jet lag"— they'd learned about it at school. "You'll feel you're traveling to the other side of the world, Daddy!" He shows the longitude which is the opposite of Beijing's; the child's thumb runs from Newfoundland past New York and south into the Caribbean, heading toward Brazil.

The father too studies the globe. There is an island so small you can scarcely make it out. *Santo Domingo*. He mouths the magic syllables. For the next three weeks his life will be synchronized with those who live on that speck of land.

"I'll be asleep when you and Mommy are awake." He realizes as he says this that this means on Sunday too.

Tingting says cheerfully, "See you in three weeks, Daddy!"

"Don't be late for school! You should go to bed right now!" says the mother and wife.

Bao tries to doze. It's difficult when sunlight is coming through the windows. He ties his wife's bra over his eyes as a makeshift blindfold . . . By midafternoon he manages to nod off . . . The alarm clock wakes him and it's dusk. He urinates, showers, puts on his work clothes, drinks and eats nothing (it's simpler and cheaper to use the cafeteria at work), and sets out. Dawn is breaking over the surf and palm trees of Santo Domingo.

He could take a bus, connecting to another bus, but he'll get there almost as quickly by walking. Why jostle on a crowded vehicle, and worry about pickpockets (seventeen years ago his wallet had been stolen) when he can rely on his own two feet? Healthful exercise; and it's the one time of day he's free, not belonging to anyone.

Beijing after dark is not so different from during the morning rush—a little cooler, yes, and the pollution is less too, he thinks. Fewer people about; we're in a smaller city, or an older one. More eye contact too: we've all been invited to the party.

He clocks in at As-You-Wish. He's just on time: the national anthem is beginning (*"Arise! ye who refuse to be slaves / From our flesh and blood, make our own Great Wall . . ."*). He takes his position at the familiar machine. (*"March forward! Forward! Forward!"*) Along with his coworkers, he performs two minutes of stretching exercises, then sets to.

His duty—as the boss's boss foretold—is identical to his regular one. He inserts a spool of wire into the machine. He presses a pedal to make the winding process start and stop. Eventually the object—one degree closer to becoming a dynamo—passes away from him along the production line. And the task is his to perform all over again.

The system is: he gets a ten-minute break at "midmorning" and "midafternoon" (i.e., just before midnight and well before dawn) plus a full forty minutes for "lunch" in the depth of night. How long does a meal take? Rice and cabbage and some meat, the same food he's been living on all these years; his sweat smells of it. A cup of tea. Then he does what he seldom did on day shift: he goes outside and watches the world.

It's warm enough, provided he wears his coat. One side of the factory faces a fairly busy intersection with a view of the raised expressway beyond: a bridge whose ends cannot be seen, a mono-chrome rainbow. He finds an abandoned seat from a car, its upholstery a faded pink; he arranges it on a pile of bricks. He balances on his throne and smokes. A puzzle runs through his head. Here's the Fifth Ring Road, and he's old enough to re-member when it didn't exist, nor the Fourth Ring Road either, and they're talking of building the Sixth and the Seventh Ring Roads, and of course there's the Third and Second, but how come there's no First Ring Road? If you start at the outside and go in and in and in, you'd expect to find it, but you never will.

And this interlude becomes his nightly custom. Always some-thing to look at (a collision of several bicycles . . . a man kissing a woman . . . a dealer on a pedal cart crying, "Recycled appli-ances!"), and the white noise of the traffic comforts him. Rarely a passerby gazes at Bao. (How must he seem to such an onlooker? Like a derelict? Like a sage on a mountaintop?) Rarer still, the passerby gestures or speaks some greeting. Bao never replies.

As Tingting predicted, he was "jet-lagged" at first, but his body soon becomes used to the schedule. One Monday he is in bed and it seems a rough hand is trying to shake him awake, but he resists, and only when he gets to work does he learn that during his sleep an earthquake has taken place, centered in a distance province. Sundays are odd. He has no son (a boy's voice cuts across his dreams). His wife is more like a mistress, who can only see him at strange hours, dressed inappropriately, on her way elsewhere. The sex is rushed and awkward, yet better than it has been for decades.

He misses the old Beijing—the daytime city—and understands now that he's always been in love with it. But he is in love with nighttime Beijing also. The glowing signs of the convenience stores, the yawning police officers, the crazies, the floozies, the punks and goths, the grave procession of shift workers like himself. Really the night city and day city are a hair's breadth apart—for all that half the world separates them.

As for what he is here for, the laboring on the factory floor, this too is almost the same as before. But not quite. In his previous existence, among his coworkers there had been a joker, a fat man called Zhurong; now the joker has a skinny mustache and his name is Chu. There had been a man who liked to pass on scurrilous gossip, just so now. In the old and new life, a drunkard. In old and new, a man who's always on about "pussy." A whiner. A fidgeter. A sports fan. A man who has opinions on politics. A grandfather. A man who's engaged. A man who sings to himself while on the job, and one who has a parlor trick— but during the day it was pop songs and now it's rock, and instead of the yo-yo he makes shapes out of pieces of string.

Further days go by, and he feels nostalgia in advance, knowing he will come to miss the night city, at the same time as he yearns to be synchronized with the daytime one. (Will he experience jet lag again, on the return flight? He guesses so.) As he heads home around dawn, he fancies he spies his other self walking in the opposite direction—a shudder as the two Baos slide through each other and continue on their ways.

Not long now till he will meet Tingting again, and tell him about the vacation. What will fit in the story? A censored version: Bao will leave out the raucous whores of Santo Domingo,

and the laughing drunkards who spill out of the bars, and the thug with an iron bar methodically smashing the windows and hood of an Audi 17. He will say, "People are the same the whole world over. They work at their jobs to make money. They love their children." He will continue, "But not everything is perfect in any country. We have migrant workers who live far from their families, and people with health problems, and people who want to marry one person but end up marrying somebody else and maybe it was for the best after all—and so do they." He will add, "And you know the street performers, Tingting, the jugglers and singers and conjurors? Well, they have performers, as good as ours." Then he'll mention the man in the underpass, just a couple of blocks from their home, who plucks traditional tunes on the erhu, "My Motherland," "Though the Candles Flicker Red," "The Flower Seller's Cry." And he'll hum to make the boy remember and smile along with his Daddy. "In Santo Domingo, there is also an erhu player. But ours is blind. And this one, he can see."

THE MOST BEAUTIFUL WOMAN IN CHINA

I

Full in her face, barbarian sands, wind full in her hair;
Gone from eyebrows, the last traces of kohl, gone the rouge from cheeks:
Hardship and grieving have wasted it away
Now indeed it is the face in the painting!

II

As the Han envoy departs, she gives him these words:
"When will they send the yellow gold to ransom me?
Should the Sovereign ask how I look,
Don't say I'm any different from those palace days!"

If the Emperor of China has never seen your face, how dare you pretend you exist. Now, there once was an Emperor who sent emissaries across the entire country to collect beautiful women and bring them back to His palace. He married all of them. He couldn't possibly invite a thousand women into the Imperial Bedchamber, so this was His system. Every evening the Grand Master of Ceremonies would set out portraits of the wives on a jade table, and the Emperor would choose from among them. The lucky woman, guarded by the Bearer of the Golden Mace and the Commander of the Five Posts, would be ushered into the Imperial Presence. If she was to His liking, she was sure to be invited back, and so she would attain a degree of privilege and power in her own right.

Out of all these women, the most beautiful and the most virtuous was Wang Zhaojun. She had grown up in Hubei in the south of the Empire, of humble stock. On her third day in the palace, the Court Portraitist, an arrogant eunuch, demanded his usual bribe. Outraged, she refused to pay. The Portraitist responded by depicting her as ugly. The upshot was that she languished in the Lateral Courts, bored and pampered, never once chosen by the Emperor.

At the time, the Emperor was engaged in negotiations with a tribe of barbarians who lurked beyond the northern frontier—the Huns. As part of a peace treaty, it was agreed that the Emperor would send the Hunnish King one of His own wives. Naturally He picked the one He believed to be the ugliest. Wang Zhaojun was escorted by the Director of Uprightness to the caravan of the Hunnish Ambassador; she was greeted with a chorus of unholy hymns accompanied by the jangling and plucking of savage instruments. The Ambassador kowtowed; he crawled backward from the Emperor. And now at last the Emperor caught sight of our heroine. The briefest of glimpses—but this was sufficient. He knew beyond doubt she was indeed the most beautiful woman in

China. Too late! He had promised her to another; the Emperor cannot break His word.

As to how the story unfolds thereafter, there are various versions . . . Wang Zhaojun lived two millennia before our time, and some eight hundred years after her death, the Tang dynasty poet, Bai Juyi, wrote the poem I have quoted above. Whether or not he imagined her fate correctly, suffice it to say, life among the barbarians must have been a sad decline for a lady who had once known the splendors of the Imperial Court, and we cannot presume a happy ending.

✻

IN MAY 2009 the romanticist Helan Xiao received an unexpected phone call . . .

Helan first came to prominence in the eighties, part of the group of writers and artists who flourished in the relative freedom that marked the reign of Deng Xiaoping. A graduate of the Foreign Studies University, she worked as an interpreter for visiting business delegations in Beijing. Her work name was "Helen," pronounced in a gamut of exotic accents. During her spare time she translated English poetry. Nineteen eighty-six was the year of her "Ode on a Grecian Urn." She was twenty-three. "Thou still unravish'd bride of quietness / Thou foster-child of Silence and slow Time . . ." Not that she lacked for offers. She was shorter than average with a darker complexion, larger breasts, narrower eyes—not particularly pretty, then, by local standards. But foreigners found her attractive. "Why not?"

they would argue. "What are you saving yourself up for, Helen?" Some tried to buy her, and one or two proposed marriage. She smiled and gave no answer, not in words at least. " 'Beauty is truth, truth beauty,'—that is all / Ye know on earth, and all ye need to know."

That winter she was in an unofficial club that met after hours in a bathhouse in Sanlitun. A heavy metal band, Panda Bear Soup, got the audience to its feet. This was followed by a theatrical skit set during an ill-defined but remote historical era. A peasant is coming home from market and he needs to urinate. (Mimed with comic effect.) For want of anywhere else, he does it in front of a Buddhist temple. He is arrested and hauled up before a judge, who fines him two taels of silver. The peasant reaches in his underwear, and pulls out a gold piece, worth the equivalent of four taels. "Excuse me, Mr. Judge, where's my change?" "Go and pee in the temple again tomorrow!" The audience, Helan included, laughed—with the exception of the man seated next to her. He looked to be in his thirties, unhip in a blue suit, his hair in a bowl cut. "I don't get it," he said in a provincial accent. He frowned and scratched his head. He informed her he was an accountant from Chengdu, by name Shao Yonghong, visiting the capital on business. The heavy metal band came back for another set, and he took out his wallet and showed her pictures of his wife and son.

When the music was done, the lead guitarist—a man in a black vinyl coat—tried to persuade Shao to invest in the band. "In the West, people like you are called 'angels.' For example, we want to smash a guitar over the amplifier, but how can we afford it?" Helan took pity on the accountant, and led him away, and they took a taxi to his hotel room, where he brought out a bottle of sorghum spirits, which she declined. She wasn't sure what made her get into bed with him—perhaps simply she was tired of being who she was. The lights stayed on. She was naked, and he was naked apart from his socks. His abacus rested on the nightstand. As he reared over her, a quotation from Deng Xiaoping came into her head, "It doesn't matter if the cat is black or the cat is white, all that matters is whether it can hunt mice." There was not much blood. At dawn they woke, and they made love again—and whereas the first time had been painful, now she took pleasure in it.

Shao's business took him to Beijing once a month. Helan discovered she had a talent for sex, at least with him. They had nothing else in common; out of bed he bored her, and in principle she considered adultery a bad idea. He tagged along with her to clubs and parties and meals in private rooms at restaurants. Her crowd tolerated him because he paid for the others— as the idiom has it, he "spat blood." When a joint was passed round, he took a toke, or several; and when later that decade heroin started coming in from the Golden Triangle, whereas she only snorted it a couple of times, he mainlined. She didn't nag him; it's not as if she were his wife. *When the Eight Immortals cross the sea, each does it in his own way.* Each month when he left her she felt relieved, yet she always took him in her arms again. In the summer of 1988 she was at the Friendship Hotel, translating at a conference on Opportunities in the Tourism Sector, and during a break she noticed Shao emerging from the men's room. He wasn't supposed to be in the hotel then; he was supposed to be in a meeting at the ministry. She could tell from his gait and manner that he'd just been shooting up. He took a pen from his pocket, and graffito'd a rectangle around the character for "man" on the sign outside, converting it into the character for "prison." In February Shao was found unconscious in the snow on Qianmen Dajie; he was taken to a hospital and then to reeducation camp. Helan was fired. She was given a low-paid, low-prestige job teaching literacy to adults. When he was released from the camp, he went back to his forgiving wife and son in Chengdu, and never again visited his lover or the fearful, sexy city of Beijing.

The poems began. The poems spilled out of her—they were in prose, not written according to any traditional canon, not coherent, at times barely comprehensible, yet she couldn't *not* write them. Everything that had happened between the two of them was in there somehow. She hardly had to censor herself. Sex, yes—at that point in history it was permissible in literature. The drugs—she didn't *describe* the search for the vein, the needle plunging in, the way a little blood seeps back, leaving a pink stain within the syringe, but the imagery, transfigured, appears in her sequence. She never wrote the word "heroin," instead alluding to "opium"—with all the weight that carries, the wars fought over it. And she inserted into her text extracts from her translation of Coleridge's poem about Xanadu; indeed the entire foreign poem—out of order, jumbled, but all there—is swallowed up in her poem. Ancient, alien fragments suddenly emerge, as if flung up by a river flowing in a deep, romantic chasm, and glimpsed through a rainbow-rich mist.

The entire hundred-page sequence was written in just thirteen days—and might have been longer, she sometimes claimed, had she not been interrupted by a person from Pingguan. In May 1989 it was accepted for publication by a small but honorable press. (It was the editor who pointed out that Coleridge's "Xanadu" is just a bizarre transliteration of Chengdu; she denied having known this when writing, consciously at least.) *A Translation, With Annotations, of "Kubla Khan or, A Vision in a Dream. A Fragment" by British Author Samuel Taylor Coleridge (1772–1834).* It sold a very respectable three thousand copies. "Weave a circle round him thrice, / And close your eyes with holy dread, / For he on honey-dew hath fed, / And drunk the milk of Paradise."

If you were around then and moved in intellectual and artistic circles, you'll remember the shock of it. Copies were passed from hand to hand. Passages were learned by heart. You can probably recite a line or two still. Surely you lusted after the author, at least in the abstract, and that kind of lust doesn't fade with the years. And didn't you identify with her too? "She's written *my* story."

Helan scarcely benefited from her reputation. She was celibate, more or less. She stayed in her one-bedroom apartment in the Xizhimen neighborhood, not far from the zoo. Though her job was poorly paid and monotonous, she took a certain pride in it. Her students were a decade or so older than herself—the generation that had missed out on conventional education, having been of school age during the Cultural Revolution. She taught them the 214 radicals, the basic 1,500 characters needed for reading and writing—or as much, anyway, as each could manage.

And so we must imagine Helan's life as laid out on the gridded page that students use for their practice: the one character to be written, again and again, by so many students, and by the teacher too, on the blackboard, showing how. And twenty years go past, and while much else changes around her, she's still in that classroom, still in that one-bedroom apartment (not yet demolished), still on the same page, still teaching students some of whom have aged along with her, though there are others young enough to be herself in 1989, still solitary (no lover, not counting certain rare, melancholy interludes), and on May 7, 2009, we hear the singing of a lovely, imaginary bird.

It was seven o'clock in the evening. She was lying on her bed, staring at the ceiling. Her daydream has been broken by the ringtone on her cellular phone (she'd downloaded the nightingale's call). The number was unknown to her.

An androgynous voice. "*Wei . . . Wei . . .* Helan Xiao? This is the Beijing Center for Classical Music. You are commissioned to write a libretto for an opera. The subject is . . . I take it you're familiar with the legend of Wang Zhaojun?"

Of course she knew the story. (During Mao's time, Wang had been held up as a symbol of the unity of the ethnic peoples of China.) She tried to picture the historical figure. What canon of beauty would have been current in the Western Han Empire during the reign of Emperor Yuan? She envisioned a shorter woman, a taller woman; paler, darker; slender, fat; with a "melon-seed" face, with a round face; with bound feet—but no, footbinding hadn't yet been invented then. She held out her own right hand, and assessed it like a sculpture—the chipped nails, the age marks, not without beauty still.

"Why *me?*"

"It's like this," said the voice (old woman? camp man? eunuch?), "Tang wants you."

"What? Who?"

"You mean you've never heard of him!" The voice sounded shocked; and then, as if quoting publicity material, "Tang Jiangnu is the leading composer of his generation! Born in Beijing, he moved to the United States in 1981, and has been living and working in North America. But now, out of love of our Motherland, he is coming back to China where the BCCM will have the opportunity of putting on his very first opera. You couldn't have a more perfect opportunity!"

"I have no experience as a librettist."

"Heavens, Ms. Helan! All I can tell you is: the composer will be hiring you personally. You'll deal direct with *him*. You're not *our* responsibility. You have an appointment to meet him at . . . let me see . . . tomorrow at two."

"But—"

She was about to protest she'd be at work then, but the phone was dead. She'd just have to get another teacher to substitute.

She slipped on her shoes and walked a couple of blocks to the nearest cybercafe. She showed her ID and signed in. The place was dim as a theater. Most of the users were teenagers playing computer games: escaping from enemies, defeating opponents, and ascending levels, before they in turn would be killed. Helan typed in the URL for her customary search engine, Baidu (literally, "Hundredfold"—its name evokes a Song dynasty poem, "Hundreds and thousands of times, for her I searched in chaos, suddenly I turned by chance to where the lights were waning, and there she stood") and its slogan gleamed on the screen: *I know you don't know what I know.* Very little turned up about the composer. A biographical note, stating he'd been born in 1958 and studied piano at the Conservatory, as well as the titles of pieces by him—all orchestral. Then she typed the Pinyin version of his name into the English-language version of Google; frustratingly she got the all-too-familiar message: "According to the local laws, regulations and policies, part of the searching result is not shown." What did she need to know about the man, anyway? If he'd been out of China that long surely she had no personal connection with him. She could only suppose he must have come across some of her poems, and found something he could use.

The Beijing Center for Classical Music is as postmodern as they come—nonrectangular windows and tilted exterior walls fabricated of some innovative material infused with red dye (the color serves to keep ghosts out, they say, or it keeps them in). It's located downtown, a stone's throw from Qianmen. The receptionist gave her a name badge to clip to her clothing and directed her to Room 3-138. She had friends who were filmmakers and painters and rock musicians and folk musicians, and had an idea of what they did, but classical music was a black hole in her knowledge. On the third floor, she passed a series of small rehearsal rooms, glass-doored but soundproofed. She saw an intense man in a white shirt, pounding on a piano in seeming silence. In another room a girl who looked to be about twelve was strumming a harp while a wizened elderly man blew and fingered his flute. A third room held nothing but a bent-wood chair with a ham sandwich on the seat. At last she reached 138. The opaque door opened and she entered.

She'd been expecting a one-on-one—but she was in a large space as busy as a classroom. The composer—the center of attention—proved to be a stocky man with bushy eyebrows and a mole (something like Mao's) at the corner of his mouth. He was simultaneously puffing away at a Marlboro Red (never mind the NO SMOKING sign on the wall), slurping coffee out of a Styrofoam cup, and talking on the telephone in English (something about frequent-flier miles) while speaking in Chinese (feng shui and absolute versus relative pitch) to a team of workmen delivering a crimson faux-leather couch and to an obviously blind man manipulating the works of a Palatino grand piano.

A final drag, a grimace that might imply disgust or super-subtle pleasure, and he disposed of the cigarette on a chopstick rest. He held out his hand with the coffee in it as if to shake hers, addressing her with startling informality, in English, "*Hey, Xiao, what's up?*"

"I'm honored to meet you, Tang Jiangnu."

The couch bearers departed and the phone call broke off. To the accompaniment of chords and discords from the tuner, the conversation continued. "So, Xiao, you'll be doing my libretto." She'd supposed a man like him would have a "musical" voice, but he spoke Beijing dialect gratingly.

"Yes, I'm looking forward to it, Tang Jiangnu."

"What's with the poker up your ass? Call me Tang. Or call me Johnny, if you like." He sidestepped, as deftly as a fencer, to inspect her from a different angle.

She couldn't possibly call him Johnny. "Very well, Tang."

"The premiere is in three months. I've pretty much done the music already, so we've just got to fit the words around it. Think you can hack it, Xiao?"

Before she could answer, the door swung open, and in swept a young, ponytailed woman graceful as a ballerina, who sang at the composer. Not "sang" in any ordinary sense—she emitted a sound which changed timbre and pitch and volume by imperceptible degrees: quiet and pure and high becoming a harmonically rich boom. Thanks to her mysterious superpowers, she did not need to breathe. Tang stood so close to her he seemed to be inspecting her mouth like a dentist. Then a woman in her thirties, glorious in a silver robe and matching tiara, sailed into the room, double-cheek-kissed the composer, and made some vociferous point about the quality and range of her own voice, in Mandarin sprinkled with English expressions and what was most likely Italian. Helan, a woman of a certain age, was used to being ignored.

At last that phase was over, and the two were alone again, not counting the blind man. Tang sipped, lit another Marlboro, killed it after a single puff, and yawned like a lion. The interior of his mouth was the least ugly thing about him. It hadn't aged (mouths don't, do they? the outside, yes, and the teeth also, but not tongue or palate?) and his dentition was that synthetic uniform kind she associated with the idea of America. He was wearing jeans, a foreign brand (though all jeans are Made in China), and a rumpled blue shirt.

She'd thought she'd taken an instant dislike to him, but on some level she must like him after all, for she yawned sympathetically.

"Let me tell you what I know about you, Xiao. You published one book decades ago, a *succès d'estime*. Since then, nothing much. Not married. No child. Some might call you a failure. Some might wonder why a man like me would choose to work with you. But what do I care? I'm successful enough for two! If you do my libretto, you'll *be* a success."

She looked him in the eye.

He went on, "All I care about is this. You can write, and you can obey my orders. Correct? Oh and by the way, your name will not be appearing on the playbill. I'll be listed as both composer and librettist. You'll be my *ghostwriter*" (using the English idiom).

She swallowed. "Two questions, Tang. How many work hours? How much money?"

He smiled. "The relationship isn't about *us*, it's about *me*. You'll be available whenever I need you. I've arranged it with your school, you won't be teaching there this summer. And I'll pay ten thousand dollars. Cash. Half up front, half on completion. Any questions?"

He was offering the equivalent of three years of her salary. Should she thank him or tell him to get lost? She felt a surge of resentment, yet she took his posturing for an act, a sign of weakness perhaps. And it's not as if she were signing a contract in her own blood; if the arrangement proved intolerable, she could always back out. Once again the door swung open and a giantess in a golden smock and with vast brilliant eyes took up position in front of the composer and launched into an eardrum-challenging recitative: "I have come from the set of *Die Walküre*! Everybody is talking about you!" Then she segued to an aria in German.

Through the open door a Gorilla wandered in. "Excuse me," it said in a Southern accent, "is this Room 3-138?"

"Yes," said Tang, and pointed at Helan.

The Gorilla sang at her, to the tune of a time-honored folk song, *"Congratulations on your new job!"* beating his chest in tempo.

Tang gave the Gorilla a tip. It left, accompanied by the strutting Valkyrie.

"Come back tomorrow, same time," Tang ordered Helan.

Meanwhile the tuner sat on the piano stool and ran through a rising scale. He bowed his head with the quiet achievement of a concert pianist.

The following afternoon Helan returned. Tang was rising to greet her when suddenly the lights blinked out and the faint hiss of the air-conditioning, never normally noticed, became evident by its absence. It was one year to the day after the Sichuan earthquake (impossible not to know; it was in all the

papers) and her instant, irrational reaction was that this was an anniversary aftershock. *Bend, not break,* she thought. *We're safe here, a long way from the epicenter.* Frowning, he banged a dissonant chord on the piano. (Strange there are instruments in the modern world independent of electricity.) He held a red envelope out to her, pushing it into her grasp—and it seemed they were in a kind of dance: they were swaying together, the building itself was, the city. "Five thousand exact," he declared. "Go and count it." She did not count, just gripped the wad of imported cash. "Let's put the agreement in writing," he said, "but how, if the printer's not working?"

"Write it by hand?"

"Yes. That's what I meant."

He put on his glasses and found a pad of paper. His calligraphy was at the level of a nine-year-old's; there were elementary errors in his characters. No doubt for decades he'd written mostly in English, and for Chinese he'd have used a computer—type in the Pinyin equivalent and the software searches for the correct character. "I'll pretty much do the libretto myself, Xiao, as well as the music," he said. "Naturally I'm just hiring you to . . ." He left the sentence unfinished, sliding his hand as if conducting an orchestra.

"Naturally," she said, and signed. Lighting reappeared; air-conditioning flowed; the Beijing Center for Classical Music resumed its canonical existence.

In the course of the first month a routine developed. Tang slept late, and was never at work before noon; he required Helan to be present most of the time he was there, usually letting her go by midnight. Her own office was in 3-139—the room adjacent to his, and glass-doored: she could see and be seen, but seldom overhear. His system was organized chaos. At the same time as the two of them were developing the libretto, he (along with the conductor and the musical director of the center) was involved in auditioning the singers—an informal process, depending, it seemed, on connections rather than simply talent. The cast had already been chosen; it was a question of deciding who would get which role, who would be the star, and who demoted to the chorus of eunuchs. (He was also dealing with the orchestra, but that was no concern of hers.)

Helan wrote for his benefit a summary of the plot, elaborating it with anachronistic detail. She recited from memory the poem by Bai Juyi, which was new to him. "Maybe we can work that in," he murmured.

"Of course we aren't restricted to that version. We could arrange for Wang Zhaojun to live happily ever after, if we want."

He grunted, "Operas always have unhappy endings, at least so far as the heroine is concerned."

But she had other duties, it turned out, making the composer coffee and cleaning his ashtrays—or whatever he used as an ashtray. A couple of times she was dispatched to pick up his laundry, and once she had to remind him to do up his fly. In addition, she served as an intermediary when requested, a Guardian of the Velvet Rope: "I'm afraid he's too busy to see anybody right now." She minded none of this, actually. She regarded her position with a measure of amusement. When all's said and done, nobody goes to the opera because they adore the libretto. Why should writing be regarded as a task more noble than emptying the trash can? Let us honor honest proletarian effort.

He played for her piano transcriptions of his proposed music. He'd already completed the score, he kept insisting, even as he considered alterations. It was a question of reordering it, to some degree, and finding words that would go with it. (She guessed there are other composers who begin with the text and set it to music. It wasn't up to her to challenge his method.) Was the music good or bad? How could anyone decide? Either way she couldn't hold it in her head.

"What's the secret of fitting words to music?" she asked. "It must be easy in nontonal languages, but in Chinese . . . I mean, suppose the syllable has a falling pitch, but your music goes up? How will the audience know what you intend?"

"Oh, nobody *listens* to the libretto these days. They just read the surtitles."

With relief more than anything she noted the absence of an erotic charge between them. Not because of his ugliness or hers (ugly people are sexy too), rather because their relationship was domestic. Once in the cafeteria she overheard that singer she'd encountered singing German, alluding to her dismissively as "Tang's *lao po*." The expression normally means "wifey," and Helan was gratified; but it can also refer to a femme lesbian, and perhaps that was the intention.

Tang was flirting, and more, with the Valkyrie. She auditioned for him in Room 3-138; afterward there were stains on the crimson couch, which Helan cleaned up with a spray can and a paper towel. For that matter he was up to something with the mezzo-soprano (the one first seen in the silver tiara). And with the third diva, too; Helan passed a supply closet and heard a repeated moan—its timbre and projection revealed it was the Ballerina's—coupled with Tang's voice saying, "*You* are the most beautiful!"

Tang was unabashed about his conquests, rubbing his belly with glee and boasting to Helan, "They're competing to be chosen as Wang Zhaojun." He stage-whispered, "They each think I'll transpose the part to fit her voice! Little do *they* know" (he stood on tiptoes and stretched his arms in a tai chi posture) "I'll be using all three! The soprano will play Wang Zhaojun when young and innocent. Then the mezzo is the Emperor's Concubine. And Wang's going to finish up as the contralto. In the final act, I want a trio with the three Wangs singing together. Can you write some lyrics for me, Xiao?"

The male singers seemed peripheral, by contrast. The two most significant were a deep-voiced, barrel-shaped, obviously gay, king of a man, Gongsun, and Ji, a tenor, a shy young man (the Hun), recently married to a charmingly plain woman in the Wardrobe Department.

Between the composer and the librettist, what happened? At the end of May he placed in her in-tray a preliminary sketch of the Act One libretto; it was in English, oddly enough. The dialogue was stilted and the plot muddled. At the time they had a mutual cold, and were sharing a box of Kleenex.

"Did you write the text yourself, Tang?"

"Not exactly . . . somebody in America . . ."

"Perhaps we could find a way to give the characters more individuality?"

"The singers have got all the individuality you could ask for, believe you me!"

"And there could be more drama in the relationships, for example when Wang meets the Eunuch?"

"Oh, Xiao!" he sneezed. They blew their noses in unison. She balled up her Kleenex and threw it, quite hard, into the can between his feet.

Over the next week she rewrote the act from scratch. Difficult to get started (she toyed with a magnetized cube where her paperclips lived, drawing forth one clip and so enticing its comrades to follow), yet once she was into it, it absorbed her. As a confessional poet she'd expressed only her own feelings:

now she was obliged to think her way into the heads of these semifictional creations, and give them speech—a vacation from being herself. The Emperor and the Hunnish King, these she pictured as rugged, romantic heros; the queens were school-girls in a dormitory getting up to pranks and japes (inspired by the British children's books she'd been assigned in advanced English); and the eunuchs were modeled on bureaucrats she'd had to deal with over the years. The craft of structuring too, shaping the interactions, she discovered she had a knack for.

She delivered her version. There and then Tang put on his gold-framed reading glasses and went through it. "It took you a whole week to make a few changes, Xiao?" he grumbled by way of appreciation. "Hey, can you do it in English too? Appeal to a broader market." (*English!?* As spoken in China two thousand years ago!?) Meanwhile the set designer delivered a maquette for the composer's approval—a doll's house model of the stage, featuring geometric forms, not evocative of any specific dynasty. Tang responded with calculated ambivalence; he ordered the designer to place the maquette in the corner like a mousetrap. Tang personally arranged a grapefruit inside it, and lit a stick of incense in front.

The fact that Tang was rude to others made it easier for her; she didn't take his lack of consideration personally. Call it a business relationship; for a boss to lord it over his underlings, that could be the American way of doing things, for all she knew. Helan was not unhappy in her role. She'd been accustomed to thinking of herself as destined to go nowhere, and not minding much, indeed being drawn to her fate—the romance of failure.

But why should this libretto be a one-off? Perhaps Tang would hire her for a future project, or some other composer would; she'd belong in the world of classical music. Or she could parlay her experience into some other personal assistant job. It's not like the old days, when you were stuck in your assigned work unit till retirement. She'd tasted fame once, and it wasn't for her; she was cut out to be an unobtrusive helper—for the likes of her, too, there is a place in modern China. This is how your life changes. You're lying flat on your back looking up at the stains on the ceiling . . . when you hear the song of a semimythical bird. What *is* a "nightingale"? She didn't know that she'd ever seen such a creature. (When translating Keats, she'd called it literally "night-bird.") Where is the expert who can inform us whether or not the nightingale exists in China?

"Why not have a scene where there's been an earthquake in a distant province, and the Emperor and his court are sending aid? It would make the Emperor a more rounded figure."

"No."

"And Wang Zhaojun is worried about the fate of her own family?"

"No."

"The audience would sympathize with the characters more. Isn't that what we're aiming for?"

"No."

On the Fourth of July the composer invited the cast to the Stars and Stripes karaoke bar in Wangfujing. Scantily dressed "little missies" brought Budweiser and juice and Jack Daniel's, and red-white-and-blue cotton candy. Tang held up his American Express card and announced everything would go on his tab. Naturally the professionals were competitive. The Valkyrie, though she couldn't *speak* English, sang phonetically, "I Will Survive." Tiara trumped that with "Je ne regrette rien," and the Ballerina, who did appear to understand the words, belted out an a capella aria from Bernstein's *Candide*. The conductor and director performed as a duet, "Take Me Home, Country Roads." Gongsun, objecting to English on ideological grounds, sang a folksong about harvesting the sorghum. Ji and his wife did something from *Cats*. And Tang surprised everyone by breaking out a banjo and accompanying himself for "Yankee Doodle Dandy."

And what about Helan? She insisted she had no voice, scarcely any voice at all. Eventually she was prevailed upon; she stumbled through the Happy Birthday Song. Everyone joined in for ". . . *birthday, Dear America* . . ." and they continued it in their own ways, in English and Chinese, straight through and harmonized, in tune and out. As she sang along with the brilliant, highly trained performers, she considered that she was the one to put words in their mouths, which they would project onstage, night after night. But for the librettist, the entire operatic enterprise could not exist.

On the fifth of July the nightingale sang again, and it was Tang's voice at the other end. He called her into his room.

He was seated at the Palatino. He was grotesque in a red T-shirt with the icon of the Olympic panda mascot, rolled up to cool his belly, baggy shorts, and knee socks. His mouth was full of sunflower seeds, and he had the knack of manipulating them with tongue and teeth, crunching the kernels and spitting the husks out on the carpet. His speech was punctuated with seed-related noises, and meanwhile his left hand harmonized in the lower register.

"Hey, Xiao. Got something to tell you. About the libretto" (his hand skipped up an octave). "We live in an age of change."

"What do you mean?"

The opening bar of Beethoven's Fifth—which he then played backward.

"Tang, I don't understand."

"The old switcheroo."

"What?"

"The traditional legend, it's too much about pictures. Visuals. Now, I've got nothing against visuals but . . . And who gives a fuck about a dead chick in the Western Han Empire anyway?"

He told her the following.

The Most Talented Violinist in China

Once upon a time, there was a woman named Wang Zhaojun. She grew up in a distant province, and she had an amazing

musical talent, and she won a place at the Beijing Conservatory. She specialized in violin. She was, in fact, the best violinist of her generation. But it's an ultracompetitive business.
The way it works, each musician makes a recording, to be
reviewed by the head of the Conservatory. Then the head picks
out the recordings he likes, which he submits to the orchestra
conductors, who audition just a few of the applicants and se-
lect from these. Now, the man whose job it was to record the
Conservatory students, he demanded a bribe from Wang. She
refused to pay. So he recorded her in such a way as to make
her sound dreadful—the worst violinist you can imagine.

Meanwhile the Chinese government was negotiating an
economic cooperation deal with an African country. China
would provide consumer goods in return for raw materials.
And to sweeten the package, China threw in some culture—
let's toss 'em a chamber orchestra. The Conservatory was
asked to supply it. Naturally the head of the Conservatory
chose the very worst musicians—Wang among them. She
had no choice. Just as she was about to leave—waiting at
the gate at Beijing airport, her flight being announced—she
took out her violin. For the first time, the head of the Conservatory himself heard her perform.

Too late! She went to Africa; and there, among the barbarians, cut off from the world of classical music, her talent languished, and she did indeed become an atrocious violinist.

Silence in Room 138.

He lit a Marlboro and pondered the burning tip.

He said ruefully, "Wardrobe Department's not going to like it, after all the work they put into period costumes. But what I say is: fuck Wardrobe!"

She thought: Is he crazy? Has he forgotten how things work here? For all that he'd spent decades away, on the surface he was Chinese. (Sure, he dropped English expressions into his conversation, but so do many people.) Wardrobe would be the least of his problems! All she could think to say was, "Why *violin*? I mean, why shouldn't the heroine play cello or, I don't know, marimba?"

He smiled graciously, showing a seed-speckled tongue. "I like composing for violin." He added, "My ex-wife was a violinist." To illustrate his point, he played a snatch of air-violin, and momentarily his face took on a feminine cast.

This was the first she'd heard of such a person; she wondered if the divorce was a motivation for leaving America.

She said, "Tang . . . Johnny. You do understand—the Ministry of Culture has approved a libretto based on the *traditional* legend?"

As if asking the piano what *it* thought, he raised his eyebrows at the keyboard. He swiveled on the stool and clasped her hand between both of his agile, plump, age-spotted ones. "My dear Xiao, all I want to know is—You *can* write it, can't you?"

She found pan and brush, and swept up the sunflower husks. She looked up at the grinning, hideous man. "Yes. I can write it—"

He told her to give him the libretto as soon as possible, and—lighting a fresh cigarette from the remains of the dying one—dismissed her with "You and I, we make a great team."

"—*but I won't.*"

It seemed he didn't hear her. Then he stared as if seeing her for the first time. "Five hundred dollars extra?"

She returned his gaze.

"A thousand?"

She was unmoved.

"If you chicken out, I'll write the libretto myself anyway, and I won't pay you a penny."

No response.

"Not for my sake, my dear Xiao, but won't you help out a poor, innocent opera?"

She wouldn't have ruled out his becoming violent when thwarted; instead disconcertingly he laughed. "When I was a lad, I was sent with my family to a commune in Guangxi Province, and classical music was forbidden. No Beethoven, no Mozart, no Brahms. We were forbidden even to think about it. I was a good little boy so I did my best to obey. I weeded the paddy field, and all the time I was doing my damnedest *not* to think about Beethoven. So guess what went through my head, all the time?" His magical hands danced and pounded on the keyboard, producing what she could only suppose to be a world-famous stretch of music. "Now, Little Comrade," he said, addressing her the way one does a child, "please try to *not* think about the libretto I have asked you to write."

That night Helan was taking the bus home from work when she saw a Gorilla on a skateboard. It was crouching, clinging to the back of a Hummer, so being drawn through the city. It wore headphones, listening to music only it could hear. In appearance it was similar to the one who'd sung for her, though who can say what kind of person was inside the costume? Perhaps she was witnessing a youth fad—like the fashion for dressing as anime characters, or the punk craze. A quarrel on the bus distracted her—a deaf-and-dumb woman bumping into a Hong Kong businessman—and when she looked out again, the Gorilla had departed. Helan smiled at her own ghostly reflection in the window, feeling affection for this Beijing of ours, always generating new stuff.

An hour or so later, the Emperor and his court entered her bedroom. En masse they kowtowed to her. *"Please help us come into existence!"* Warriors and eunuchs along with the many beautiful queens, all apologized for how they'd mistreated her and undervalued her over the years. She became aware they were addressing her as Wang Zhaojun. *"Actually my name is . . ."* But the distinction was a slight one, and in any case it was hard to keep up rational conversation now that Emperor and courtiers and queens had crawled close, and were kissing and caressing every inch of her body.

Helan was hard at it. She sat in 3-139, scribbling away like a demon. How could she help herself? If she resigned, Tang would come up with his own libretto, inadequate as it might be, and she'd be tainted by association anyway. Grudgingly she respected him for sticking to his principles, though it was unclear what his principles were. Besides, as he'd foreseen, she couldn't resist the opportunity; the words flocked into her head, eager to be written down. What made it possible for her was the thought that this was her own work, but *not* her own. It was delusional to suppose it would ever be approved for performance, but it wasn't *her* delusion.

As she wrote, the characters in her libretto came alive for her. A double vision: their world was the real one yet also her invention. She marveled at the fact of existing in Beijing in 2009. Treating herself, she'd go on mini-excursions to far-flung regions of the center—peeking into the fifth floor bookkeeping office, and into Wardrobe (contrast between the soberly dressed women who worked there and the hung-up ranks of gorgeous costumes), and down to the basement recreation room, its Ping-Pong table unofficially requisitioned by the percussion section. With a sigh of satisfaction she'd return to her little room, her libretto.

By the end of the week she had a complete draft, and she brought it around to 138. The room had an exterior window like a rhomboidal porthole, and the city beyond (she noted with mild astonishment) was bewitched by a summer storm—purple clouds crazed with lightning flashes, and unheard thunder; the streets awash, the urban colors deepened. A pigeon, its wings extended, hovered outside the porthole.

The composer himself was at the piano, playing a chord sequence, another one, and yet another, crossing out the score, scrawling in the margins. It was long seconds before he acknowledged her presence. "I'm reworking the orchestration. I want to make Western instruments sound like guqin and pipa. It'll be hell for the string section."

She stayed by the door, her creation in her arms. She opened her mouth, intending to register her protest. "I'm not sure about—"

"Yes?"

"I'm not sure about the title," she said. "Should we rename the opera *The Most Talented Violinist in China*? But how *can* we? The publicity material has already gone out."

"The original title stays! If she's the best violinist, then she *is* the most beautiful!"

He beckoned her closer, thumb on middle finger, index finger wagging. "Here, Xiao. Give me."

He jumped up and took the sheaf of paper—and improvised a fan dance with it, preposterous and graceful.

Within twenty-four hours he showed her his reworking. It was evident that written language was almost as alien to him as classical music was to her: he was thinking of the text as pure sound, hardly bothering with the meaning. He gave her back her own words, but reduced, simplified, transformed—often a single phrase would be repeated several times, or sung by different performers. Now she knew he'd been bluffing (subconsciously she must have known this all along), he never was capable of writing his own libretto. Too late now for her to back out; the collaborative process enthralled her at the same time as she pitied herself for doing his will; she was addicted. She made further revisions, and so did he; printouts shuttled to and fro. She was co-composer of the music too, so it felt— the way you might dream you are conversing in a language that in reality you don't understand.

Once she entered his room to discover him in the process of changing his T-shirt. Poorly coordinated, he struggled, the thing pulled up like a mask over his face, his belly aquiver. He was humming the "Ode to Joy." She thought of the monster, Xing Tian, who even after his head had been cut off in battle did not cease wielding his sword, "seeing" with his nipples and "breathing" through his navel. She valiantly resisted her yearnings to stab him through the heart with her ballpoint and to tickle him till he apologized.

By the end of July they had a final draft. They leafed through the score, words and music together—proud parents. She loved this opera, and supposed he did too, all the more so because it was destined never to be performed, the way you might care for a disabled child who could never go out into the world. He said gruffly, "The singers have a full month to get it down pat. No problem. They're professionals."

She noticed that in the cafeteria no one sat next to her. Quietly alone she ate her salad and rice, from time to time turning the pages of a Ming dynasty erotic novella. The cast, the orchestra, the administrative staff—they all shunned her as if she were infectious. They even avoided getting in the same elevator car with her, an effect enhanced by the fact that the chorus, protective of their vocal chords, wore surgical masks, the way everyone had done during the SARS crisis. The only person who had any time for her was Tang, and he didn't have much. "Do me an English version, please," he said casually. "I asked you a while ago. Why don't people do what they're told?"

"You know, the rule is, for literary translations, the translator does it *into* her mother tongue."

"Who cares? Just do it."

She did.

At the beginning of August a delegation arrived at her room. It was the three singers who'd be playing Wang Zhaojun. They filed inside, in order of seniority: the Valkyrie, the Tiara, and the Ballerina. With an instinctive sense for visual composition, they arranged themselves like figures painted on an urn, or like the Peasant, Physician, and Intellectual on the old fifty-yuan bill.

"We beg you . . . ," said the Valkyrie.

"*We go down on our knees and beg you . . . ,*" said the Tiara (not literally doing anything of the sort).

"WE BE-E-E-E-EG YOU . . . ," blasted the Ballerina.

"Don't be so stubborn . . ."

"*Stubborn . . .*"

"STUBBORN . . ."

"If you persist . . ."

"*If you insist . . .*"

". . . ON YOUR FUCKING LIBRETTO . . ."

". . . the opera . . ."

". . . *will be banned . . .*"

". . . BANNED."

And, to her amazement, from the right eye of the Valkyrie, flowing down her cheek, appeared one perfect tear . . .

. . . *tear* . . .

. . . TEAR.

How could Helan respond? She sympathized. But was *she* the one who'd decided to update the plot? Was *she* "wearing the big hat"? "When I came to the BCCM," she said, "I hoped to learn about classical music. Now I understand how little I know."

Exit divas.

Beside her desk there was an upright piano, a Pearl River. For the first time she lifted the lid. Her fingers brushed over the keys, the white and the black, making no sound. Why was Tang hell-bent on self-destruction anyway—a lone figure standing in front of a column of tanks? For the sake of defending artistic integrity? Or to oppose corruption, or Chinese policy in Africa? Truly there's nothing scary about defeat—what is terrible is to suffer for an ignoble cause.

Two days later she was in 138, stapling photocopies of the score, and Tang was hunched on the piano stool slurping a bowl of instant noodles. The phone rang, and she picked it up.

"Tang Jiangnu's office."

"I'm calling from the Ministry of Culture. Might I speak to—"

"I'm Tang Jiangnu's personal assistant. Perhaps I can help you?"

He mouthed *Who is it?* She covered the receiver with her hand and mouthed the reply.

He sprinted over on Adidas sneakers and grabbed the phone from her hand. With a grand wave and glare, he shooed her from the room. His mouth rich with noodles, he mumbled urgently, "Tang here. What's up?"

That evening he invited everyone who mattered at the center to a banquet at a restaurant by Houhai Lake. She didn't have anything special to change into, but she let her hair down, and she applied a touch of blemish concealer and—why not?—lipstick. She took a moment to review herself in the women's room mirror. Her sleepy-looking eyes seemed not unappealing, and her breasts cheated gravity in the uplift bra; shy illiterates were always falling in love with her. Tang was neatly dressed for a change, in collared shirt and tan corduroy jacket. The two of them took a cab together, flowing with the traffic past the measureless expanse of Tiananmen Square and turning north, and arrived before dusk. It was strange being in the open air at this time of day—she'd been indoors for so long. Beijing in high summer, the sweaty heat and the smog so thick you could slice it. The maître d' guided Helan and Tang through to a private room, where the chandelier was crystal and the wallpaper seemed fashioned of gold leaf. They sat side by side at the circular table. Tang placed a little cup on the lazy susan and filled it with tea, and spun the thing, passing her the tea the long way around.

They were the only ones present.

The air-conditioning was powerful, and goose bumps rose on her arms.

They waited half an hour, and still nobody else showed up.

Tang clicked his fingers at the waiter like a hypnotist waking a volunteer from a trance, and ordered enough food for a dozen. As the successive dishes were brought in, he said of each, "This is my favorite!" She contemplated him tucking into the goose head and the duck feet and the frog with peppers and the blood tofu and a stir-fry of chicken with potato and the braised cauliflower. He ate as if he would never eat again; and she quietly drank a little soup and dipped her chopsticks in several dishes, taking just enough so as not to seem ungrateful. In the background there was Muzak, which she was oblivious to—until he said, "Don't you just *hate* it when they do that?" and she intuited what he was referring to; and yes, now she listened, she did dislike it too. *Heard melodies are sweet, but those unheard are sweeter.*

She murmured, "The idea to make an opera about Wang Zhaojun, the original suggestion came from . . . ?"

"My ex-wife, yes." He was gazing in Helan's direction but not at her. She imagined a Sinophile American—watery blue eyes and one of those names like Jennifer—pining for her husband's attention.

There was a pause in the conversation, which was eventually filled with small talk—about traffic, pollution, the Olympics that had taken place a year before and already felt like ancient history. He said, "You know Beijing pretty well, don't you?" A rare compliment; or else he was lamenting his own relative ignorance. What is a city other than its people—from illiterates to divas, dissidents to multinational executives, high-ranking cadres to poets?

She said, "You're right." She saw herself from his point of view: a figure to be exploited, but also knowledgeable, peculiarly talented, indispensable. She popped a choice morsel of frog into her mouth.

"The Gorilla's late," he cut into her thoughts.

"What?"

"I hired him to sing you the Retirement Song." He tapped at his BlackBerry and put it on speaker phone. "Find out what's going on."

She found herself addressing a representative of a bicycle courier company.

"Oh, *him*," said a female voice, with the scolding intonation of a Beijing "auntie." "The Gorilla went AWOL. You just can't get reliable employees these days."

"Go hunt him down!" Tang said, "Or get a replacement! It's important! You've still got the Gorilla costume, haven't you?"

"Ha! We keep hiring new couriers and they keep vanishing. Now if you know where to find a legal resident with a work permit, willing to bike around the city dressed like a monkey, and who can sing loud and clear, you just send him right along!"

Tang called for the check. He put on reading glasses and verified the total, which he paid, tipping appropriately, and they emerged into the evening, which had become hazy and gentle, no longer intolerably hot (this is what those people who love summertime in Beijing love). Young couples were walking hand in hand and pimps were touting for business. A street of upside-down restaurants was suspended in the dark lake. *Here lies one whose name was writ in water.* A busker played an achingly famil-iar tune on the erhu, over and over again. The composer and the librettist walked together to the intersection, where he waved down a taxi, and she set off to catch her bus. Then—as in a dream—he was back, running after her, shouting her name, and he put his arm on her arm, and he gave her one final, notional peck on the lips, along with a red envelope containing sixty one-hundred-dollar bills.

The following day Helan came back to pick up her stuff, such as it was. The center was eerily quiet. She passed a succession of empty rehearsal rooms. The news of the cancellation, though expected, had power to stun. A few hunched figures stumbled around carrying stringed instruments, as if hired to play at a wake.

Just as she was leaving, she heard a voice coming from a booth recessed behind the reception desk. "*Wei . . . wei . . .* Beijing Center for Classical Music. How can I help you?" She recognized the voice as that of the androgyne who'd summoned her here; the blind piano tuner was seated at the switchboard. She gazed at him—the oval of his face, the eyes which were no more than a pair of smudged dents below the brow—getting her fill.

✳

SHE RESIGNED her teaching job. The money meant she didn't need to work for a good while. She asked herself what she was now capable of. She stayed home. For twenty-four hours, she didn't eat, didn't sleep. She put pen to paper. What came out was not poetry but prose, and not in a feverish ecstasy of inspiration but steadily—so she created the barely fictionalized lives of people in Beijing. Each chapter was a mere strand, but together they formed an intricate skein, a world. To give herself courage, she pretended a foreign author had made up these stories—a tall, handsome, courteous man—and she was translating him into Chinese. As the writing progressed, she reversed the fantasy: the foreigner humbly requested the right to translate her own work into English and to publish it under his name, to give her an international audience along with the blessing of anonymity.

Some weeks later she found time to search for Tang on the Internet; however, relevant sites remained blocked. So she contacted an old friend of hers, Pan Qing, who'd played guitar in Panda Bear Soup. The band had performed for the demonstrators in Tiananmen in May 1989; after the events of June he'd fled to Hong Kong. A year later he returned. He kept his head down and worked as a software developer; now he ran a business outsourcing Chinese programming expertise. He invited her round to his place in Zhongguancun. When Helan entered his home, his pretty, much younger wife was on the couch with their two-year-old daughter on her lap, watching a cartoon on TV. Pan and Helan had slept together a few times, back in 1989 when the revolution was about to begin. She wondered if his wife suspected, but why would it even cross her mind?

"Helan Xiao is a writer," he introduced her. "She's famous for her contribution to *The Most Beautiful Woman in China*."

"Oh," the wife said, impressed. "Isn't that a reality show?" And in a sterner voice, "She needs to be changed. I'll take her upstairs." The child had begun whimpering.

Pan led Helan through to his study overlooking the garden. He tapped the keyboard, awakening his desktop. "See, the way I get through to blocked sites, I download a proxy server. It seems like I'm accessing the Web from another country. The proxy runs a bit slow, sometimes."

He clicked through to the *Wikipedia* for Tang Jiangnu. "Is this *it*?"

What was remarkable was what was *not* there. There was a complete list of the performances of Tang's work, and his career up to whenever the *Wikipedia* had last been revised, some months ago. Over the previous two decades, less than a dozen works of his had been heard in public, all of them at venues in small North American cities. He'd taught piano and composition at several community colleges and at a university extension. Far from being an internationally successful composer, he'd struggled, barely getting by. Only in China was he "famous in America."

Now Pan clicked on Google News. Headlines blared out. From AP and the BBC and the *New York Times*: BANNED IN CHINA . . . COMPOSER CENSORED BY BEIJING . . . "THE LEADING CHINESE COMPOSER, TANG JIANGNU, WHOSE OPERA *THE MOST BEAUTIFUL WOMAN IN CHINA* WAS BANNED BY THE CHINESE GOVERNMENT, WILL HAVE HIS WORK PREMIERED AT THE METROPOLITAN OPERA IN THE COMING SPRING SEASON . . ." There was news, too, that the production would move subsequently to Houston and San Francisco and the Opéra Bastille. His next opera, tentatively entitled *The Monkey King in the Context of Globalization*, was commissioned by the Salzburg Festival.

Why shouldn't she wish him well? She could hardly dare suppose that he missed her. He could never return to China. Was he in exile, then? Or was he now American, and China was for him the land of the barbarians? For herself, she'd never visited another country and doubted she ever would; let the world come to Beijing.

Pan intuited, "You and Tang, were the two of you . . . ?"

She colored. "Oh, nothing like that. Just . . . we were a great team."

He patted the chair next to him, and she sat down. There's a variant of the Wang Zhaojun legend in which she's happy among the Huns, grateful for the fate that brought her to this unexpected place. Helan confided her project; he agreed with her plan to have the book published under a foreign pseudonym, just in case. She described the chapter she was working on, about a singer in a gorilla suit. He joked she should do that job herself, to gather material. "But I *could* do it!" she laughed along with him, "I could do many things."

ACKNOWLEDGMENTS

Helan Xiao would like to thank Jonathan Tel, "without whom . . ."

☆

Jonathan Tel gratefully acknowledges residencies at the Mac-Dowell Colony and the Blue Mountain Center. He thanks Elizabeth Hollander for ongoing editorial advice; Nat Sobel and Julie Stevenson; Judith Gurewich, Mimi Winick, and the team at Other Press; Burton Watson for his inspired translation of the poem by Bai Juyi; Silvia Fomina for enticing him to become an opera librettist; Laura Pooley for joie de vivre; Jonathan Shock for discussions of string theory and Beijing cuisine; Will Moss for enlightenment on the workings of Chinese capitalism; Nicky Chang for a Shanghai perspective on Beijing; Fay Chan for a Hong Kong perspective on Beijing; Ho Lin for evoking Beijing in San Francisco, Dan Friedman for evoking Beijing in New York, and Amy Lee for evoking Beijing in Vancouver; and, above all, the inhabitants of Beijing.